Also by Patricia Martz Heyer:

13 Ghostly Tales and Yarns of the Navesink:
Where History and Folklore Collide.

Ghostly Tales of Two Rivers

Curious Encounters Along the Navesink and Shrewsbury Rivers.

Patricia Martz Heyer

Patricia Martz Heyer

Dedicated to my husband, Bob.
Without his encouragement and support
I would have no tale to tell.

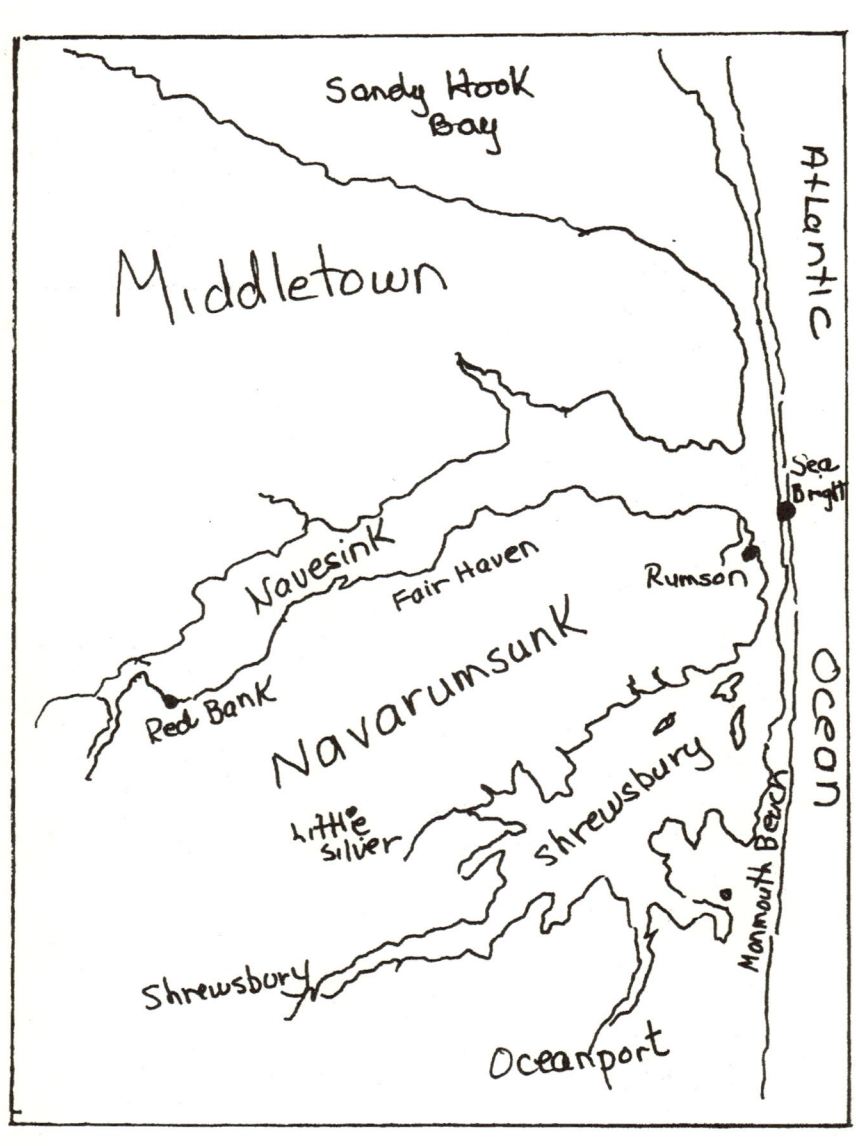

Introduction

Ghostly Tales of Two Rivers is a collection of folktales, unexplained events, and ghostly encounters emanating from the shores of our sister rivers, the Navesink and the Shrewsbury. These accounts have been harvested from a variety of historical archives, out of print publications, oral histories, and shared folklore. The detailed historical background for each tale not only enriches the story line but also provides the reader with a clear frame of reference for the historical event and its consequences.

The setting for these ghostly encounters is our beautiful twin rivers, the Navesink and the Shrewsbury, and the peninsula they create. The Lenape referred to this land as Narvarumsunk. But for most of us, it is simply home. The five-mile-long and three-mile-wide peninsula includes the towns Red Bank, Fair Haven, Rumson, Little Silver, Monmouth Beach, and parts of Middletown, and Shrewsbury. As the barrier beach serves as a border to our East, and is connected by several bridges, we include Sea Bright and the remaining barrier beach from Monmouth Beach to Sandy Hook.

The local historical record for the two rivers and the peninsula offers evidence of the numerous and noteworthy contributions of this area in the history of our nation. It was here in our very back yard that democracy was born. It was here the evils of slavery sprouted into a Civil War. Here in our little corner of the world that the decade long civil disobedience against Prohibition would be waged. Here the budding steamboat era blossomed, here the newly developing railroad expanded, and Here the industrial revolution evolved into the age of technology. Throughout it all America has relied on these two rivers, the peninsula, and the good people who call this place home. These two marine estuaries and their peninsula, Narvarumsunk, have contributed to and celebrated America's successes; as well as suffering the heartbreak of her tragedies.

At the same time the number of both written and oral reports of local paranormal activities has remained consistently elevated over the years. Much has been written about why there is so much paranormal and inexplicable activity in the area. Some authors claim it is the intense history of the area that stimulates the innumerable number of supernatural claims. Others insist that this connection with history couples with our close affiliation with the ocean resulting in incalculable amounts of spontaneous energy in our area. They contend that the tremendous energy resulting from the Atlantic being the graveyard of the sea somehow fuses our historic energy resulting in what some call a numen, a place which has a spiritual or mystical energy of its own. Whatever the cause, we know there are countless records of apparitions, ghostly encounters, unexplained events, and peculiar sightings across our region.

It is from these unique circumstances that the stories of Ghostly Tales of Two Rivers: Encounters along the Shrewsbury and Navesink Rivers have been gleaned. They are chronicles unique to this location, and to our neighbors who have shared them with us. Within these pages you will be introduced to the numerous forms of ghostly specters you are likely to encounter here. You will meet spirits who refuse to leave, ghosts with unfinished business, specters who just want to say good bye, and some who just do not realize they are dead.

There are accounts of apparitions floating on the Shrewsbury as well as those frozen in the ice of the Navesink. There are unique and singular paranormal accounts of the Prohibition era, and the peculiar accounts of a successful, yet seemingly haunted farm that once thrived along the Shrewsbury. You will visit cemeteries where the dead are not always at rest, and a trilogy of gruesome specters and ghouls who invaded the Old Middletown Village.

These curious encounters found along the Shrewsbury and Navesink are thought-provoking, yet absorbing reading. They not only highlight our colorful history; but also link with the unrestrained energy of the human spirit, exposing the intersection of history and the paranormal all around us. So, kick off your shoes, get comfortable, and read on to learn more of the ghostly tales of our two rivers.

Table of Contents

Ghosts of the Two Rivers Peninsula

The Two Rivers peninsula, known to the Lenape native Americans as Navarumsunk, is that five-mile-long and three-mile-wide stretch of land that separates the Navesink on the north and the Shrewsbury on the south. Located to the East alongside the two merging estuaries is a narrow barrier beach which stretches from Sea Bright to Sandy Hook. It is undoubtedly one of the most historic and beautiful spots in all of New Jersey; made even more special because it is our home.

Much has been written about our little neck of the woods in both history books as well as travel brochures. Just as we have welcomed countless visitors to our rivers and shores, so too have we experienced a history that is unparalleled in intensity and richness. Who else can claim that the great battle for freedom and liberty was fought in their own back yards? We can. Not only was our region the epi center for American independence, but also served as the grocery store for Union troops during the Civil War. We can't forget that it was our shores which served as the final strategic line of defense during two world wars.

This peninsula has indeed an extremely rich and colorful history, and so it is not surprising that it also has a rich chronicle of paranormal activities, which includes a host of ghostly sightings. It is not a new phenomenon; local people have shared personal paranormal accounts by word of mouth for nearly four centuries. Ever since the beginning of the eighteenth century numerous individuals have written their accounts into the historical record. The archives are full of accounts of apparitions, manifestations, phantoms, and ghostly encounters along the banks of our twin rivers.

Admittedly, some attempt to explain away their experiences claiming a natural cause. But there are those incidents for which we just don't have an answer. Anecdotes have been told and retold, and hauntings and sightings documented. At last people are sharing their supernatural accounts of life along the twin rivers. But what kind of supernatural events are we talking about?

We are talking about the most commonly known and discussed of all paranormal experiences, ghosts. We're exploring those spirits that haunt the rolling green banks of the Navesink and the scenic marshy slopes of the Shrewsbury and that land in-between known as Navarumsunk, the peninsula.

So exactly what is a ghost? The answer to that depends largely on who you ask? Dictionary.com says that a ghost is," the soul of a dead person, a disembodied spirit imagined, usually as a vague, shadowy or evanescent form, as wandering among or haunting living persons." That says it concisely, yet if you asked a hundred different people the same question you will likely get nearly a hundred different answers. At the same time, we all have a general agreement that ghosts are spirits of those deceased. We refer to them by a variety of names such as: ghosts, spirits, apparitions, specters, phantoms, spooks, wraiths, banshee, shadows, or phantasms.

We will not likely be able to all agree on who or what they are, where they came from, where they are going, and most of all, why we see them? The theories, explanations, and hypothesis are as varied as there are experts.

Spiritualists would say that the human spirit survives after death and that ghosts are the souls of those deceased individuals who for some reason have not passed on to the next plane of existence.

Those with a great affinity for physics claim that it was Einstein that explained how ghosts can exist. This theory insists that to understand ghosts we must understand that the universe and everything in it is energy.

Einstein stated that "Energy cannot be created or destroyed; it can only be changed from one form to another." So, when a human dies his energy cannot just dissipate, it must go somewhere. By definition then that energy which has departed the human body moves into another dimension of time or space.

There are countless explanations and theories about the origins or even definitions of a ghost. We can leave that debate to the philosophers, scientists, and theologians. What we do know for certain is that a belief in ghosts and spirits has been part of the human condition since the beginning of recorded history. They have been identified on every continent of the globe, in every world culture, both ancient and modern. They are part of nearly every religion, philosophy, and folklore. (Even those without a concept of an afterlife.) We only need to glance at our society's fascination with the supernatural as evidenced by the number of movies, television shows, magazines, and books, to know that twenty first century humans are entranced by tales of ghostly specters.

What sort of specters are we likely to meet here along our riverbanks and shores? One thing most students of the supernatural agree upon is that not all ghosts are alike. It is a given that all ghosts are deceased. Just as with the living, individual ghosts have specific characteristics which makes each one unique.

Certain kinds of ghosts make only one appearance; some are with us constantly. Some make no effort to communicate, some can't stop making noises. Some are obviously aware of their situation as ghosts, others think they are still living. Some have agendas for their visits; others randomly come calling. Some ghosts are loving and fun, some are mean and scary. It takes all kinds.

One thing, most experts agree on is that there are two forms of spirit life. Human and non-human. In addition, they insist there is calendar of sorts which ghosts follow. It may be confusing for us, as they do not use 365 day per year Gregorian calendar. But their timetable does intersect ours, creating specific dates when ghostly appearances are more likely to occur.

The cluster of ghostly specters we find along our riverbanks and shores fall into six broad categories. We'll explore these groupings to identify their unique characteristics and then meet some of these specters with whom we share the peninsula.

Group 1: Intelligent / Interactive ghosts

As you travel throughout the two rivers region this is the ghost you are most likely to encounter. These spirits demonstrate intelligence and have the ability to interact with humans. They may manifest as historical figures, family loved ones, or even intimate friends who have passed on. Frequently they exhibit the same personality they had in life, and demonstrate a wide range of emotions.

These specters are anxious to make their presence known to humans. They do this by speaking, singing, making noises, and sometimes being visible. Often, we know this ghost is nearby from its lingering scent. The specter's favorite cologne, cigar or pipe smell, even the aroma of specific foods can identify the spirit and let us know it is nearby.

The guardian angel is a specific kind of intelligent ghost. This spirit with its bright aura is closely aligned with God, and exhibits a strong positive energy. This spirit tends to linger near loved ones or appear to offer aid to those in distress. They watch out for, and offer comfort throughout their lives to those they encounter. Some make their presence known, others remain invisible; yet the individual may feel that someone is looking over his shoulder in a kind and loving way. Although most people assume this is a deceased ancestor or close friend, guardian angels have been known to be former care givers and first responders such as policemen, firemen, teachers, nurses, and pastors.

Another member of interactive ghost category is the clan spirit. These intelligent spirits are attached to specific families. They remain with that particular family for many generations. They are likely considered part of the family, and frequently warn the family of coming calamities. We hear of a few attached to older American families, but they are widely accepted in Scotland, Ireland, and England.

These intelligent spirits have been recorded in significant numbers here in the water shed region of the two rivers. Many accounts involve

Intelligent ghosts which are anxious to let you know they are here. The pleasantness of their visit depends on the personality of the ghost.

3 Boys and a House Possessed: A Red Bank Haunting

Just a few doors down Front Street near the Washington Street Historic district in Red Bank once stood a creepy old haunted house. Well, that is what the fifth graders at the nearby Mechanic street school would have told you.

The two-story white clapboard house had a wide wraparound porch, tall narrow windows, dark shutters, and a pair of paneled front doors. There was nothing specular about the house except for its delightful view of the Navesink. The house was nestled between a similar home on its left, a funeral home on the right, and along its back yard fence the Mechanic Street School. The house is gone now, torn down in the late 1960's to make way for a yellow brick medical building.

The last resident of the house was an old woman who lived there all alone for many years. All the children knew of the woman was that she was old, was stingy with candy on Halloween, and was therefore likely a witch.

By the early 1960's the house had fallen into disrepair. The sidewalk was cracked, and the yard overgrown with quack grass and weeds. The faded black shutters hung at odd angles off the side of the front windows. The paint had long since chipped and faded, leaving the house appearing weather worn and shoddy.

The house stood vacant for quite some time. Before long the abandoned building became a nuisance in the neighborhood and an attraction to vagrants and local kids. The old woman's property had never been claimed so it remained there along with what appeared to be her hoarder's collection of paper bags, magazines, old stuffed animals, and dolls. It wasn't long before the rumor spread that the old lady had indeed been a witch and had left a curse on the house. If anyone entered the upstairs bedroom where she died they would never be able to utter a word of what they had seen.

The principal at the school, Miss McCue, admonished the students

5

regularly about trespassing on the property. Any student seen on or near the property was immediately sent up to Miss McCue for a serious talking to.

But fifth grade boys being fifth grade boys, found this a challenge they could not resist. It began as game of dare and double dare. At first, they would dare one another to just climb the porch steps. Once they had achieved that feat, the dares progressed to knocking on the door. From there it advanced to pushing open the door, and finally to stepping inside the house into the long dark hallway.

The house itself was laid out like many of its period. You stepped from the front door into a wide entrance hall. Along one side a narrow wooden staircase led to the second-floor bedrooms. On each side of the hall was a room connected to the hallway by matching sets of double doors. At the very end of the hallway was a kitchen and larder.

The old house continued to entice the children, despite stern lectures from Miss McCue and dire warnings from their parents. It wasn't long before three fifth grade boys became brave enough to push open the front door and peer inside. All it took was one dare after another, followed by a double dare or two, and the trio was well on their way to bragging rights about having been inside the old house.

One afternoon the three boys, Kip, Willie, and James decided it was time to investigate the old house once and for all. They agreed they would first search the rooms downstairs, and then they would all go upstairs and see for themselves the room where the old witch had died.

Being good Boys Scouts they each came to school that day prepared with a folding scout knife and a flashlight. Each boy had told his mother he was staying after school for extra help with his math. (Everyone knew how difficult long division with decimals could be.) When the dismissal bell rang, the trio headed straight for the old house.

It was a dreary day, gray clouds covered the sky, and the air was still and cold. When they got to the front door they glanced around to be sure no one was watching. Kip leaned against the heavy door and it swung opened with a great creak. Willie stepped inside, and glanced around. Before he could take another step, Kip and James piled in behind him, bumping him from behind sending the trio sprawling against the side wall.

Just then the front door slammed shut with a loud bang. The boys scrambled to their feet. "That's not funny!" someone muttered. They looked at one another wide eyed, each accusing the other of slamming the door.

Willie, who was a bit taller, and therefore considered himself the leader, turned on his flashlight and led the others farther into the hallway. It was a wide entrance with an old patterned tile floor. They used their flashlights to trace the cobwebbed molding across the high ceiling, and to illuminate each corner of the room one by one. Finally, they stood at the bottom of the old wooden stairs and aimed their lights on the dusty steps that led to the second floor.

"Come on," Willie urged, as he led them into the room to the right of the stairs. He pushed open the set of double doors that led into the room. It might have once been a dining room, but it was hard to tell. There wasn't much furniture, for the room was filled with clutter of all kinds. The ceiling light dangled on a lone wire. There were bags and cardboard boxes overflowing with what looked like old clothes, stacks of yellowed magazines, and a bunch of very dusty old stuffed animals. Most were missing their eyes, and the boys agreed that they smelled like old socks.

Coughing and mumbling the boys followed Willie across the hall into the other room. This looked more like a living room, as there was some old furniture stacked up against a dusty and cluttered fireplace mantel. They flashed their lights across the room and into each corner. Everywhere they looked it was the same, more boxes, bags, magazines, and more eyeless stuffed animals and a few dolls, some of which were missing their arms or legs.

Just then the patter of footsteps overhead stopped them dead in their tracks. The boys stood motionless, staring at one another. Willie put his finger to his lips to gesture, "Be quiet." Again, the footsteps echoed just above their heads.

The footsteps stopped, but in its place the wind began to beat on the sides of the house with the intensity of a hurricane. When James asked, "What is that?" The others could hardly hear him. Willie peered out the front window onto Front Street. The trees stood perfect straight, there was not even a breeze flapping the leaves. Yet the howling wind continued.

They returned to the center hallway and stood at the bottom of narrow wooden stairs. There were several deep breaths, and at least one audible gulp. "Let's go," Willie said as he charged up the stairs. With each step the staircase creaked and groaned. Kip followed close behind holding tightly to the dusty bannister.

Close on his heels came James, stepping gingerly on each tread. "Look a footprint!" he gasped.

The other two laughed," You jerk, those are our footprints!"

James took a deep breath, muttering to himself, "Oh, yea."

Without warning a cold wind swept down the staircase engulfing the boys in an icy mist. They instantly began to shiver. Then the doors to the downstairs rooms slammed shut with a loud boom. With that James bolted! He leapt from the stairs, landing on the floor just inside the front door. He pulled on the latch and was out on the porch before Willie or Kip could respond.

Kip and Willie looked at one another. Then Willie called out," Cluck, cluck, cluck! James is a chicken, cluck, cluck, cluck." At that moment, the front door once again slammed shut and a booming laughter echoed through the house. The two stood frozen about half way up the stairs. It was then they noticed that the wind had died down, in fact it had stopped howling altogether. As they moved up another step along the staircase Kip noticed that the very walls of the house were moving. The wall along the staircase seemed to fill with air and expand. Just when the boys thought the wall would burst, there was an audible exhale as the walls shrank back to normal.

"I'm out of here!" Kip cried as he ran back down the stairs. He jerked on the front door knob, for a long moment it did not move. Then ever so slowly the great door swung open. Kip dashed through the opening to the safety of the porch.

Willie was left alone in the old house. He was nearly to the top of the stairs. Should he escape with the others, or take a few more steps and see what was in that bedroom? The only sound he heard was the sound of labored breathing coming from the nearby wall. He reached the landing and as he turned to his right, every door in the house slammed open and shut again; except for the one bedroom door Willie was facing. There was an audible chuckle and the bedroom door swung open, and Willie walked inside.

No one knows exactly what happened to Willie that day in the deserted bedroom in the old house. When he ran out the front door a few minutes later his eyes were wide, sweat poured down his face, and tears dribbled down his cheeks. When asked what happened he could only stutter, "It, it, it…" Willie never again spoke of the old house to anyone, not even his two best friends. And although Willie had never stammered before that day, he continues to do so to this very day.

Group 2: Crisis Specters

This genre of ghost usually makes a one-time appearance. It usually appears when the individual is in true crisis or under great emotional stress. During this appearance, the spirit may be coming to say goodbye or to offer comfort to the loved one who is mourning.

In some cases, we might see the apparition of a loved one at a very specific time of day, such as precisely noon. The image suddenly disappears and you learn later than the friend died at that exact hour. Other times the crisis ghost appears when one is near to death. The spirit may be a sibling, parent, or other loved one who arrives to help the person to cross over.

These apparitions are frequently observed during traumatic situations such as combat, surgery, horrific accidents, grisly murders, and terrorist attacks. They seldom appear more than three days after the individual's death. Large numbers of such sightings were recorded during both World Wars as well as Vietnam.

A related form is the anniversary ghost. This specter appears on the anniversary of a date that was important to him when alive, perhaps the day of his death, or the date of the birth of a child.

Yet another form of crisis specter is popularly known as the phantom. This modern-day ghost can be easily confused with a living person. These spirits seem to be solid; they dress and act in a normal manner. They have been regularly reported in bus terminals, on highways, and airports. It is not unusual to see such phantoms walk through security stations totally unnoticed.

The classic account of this sort of phenomena is the tale of the hitchhiker who is picked up on an isolated highway. The young man seems normal in every way, from his jeans and tee shirt to his love of modern music and disheveled hair. When they reach the truck stop both the driver and the hitchhiker walk together into the restaurant. The driver leads the way to the counter and orders two cups of coffee. He reaches to pass the sugar to the hitchhiker, he has vanished. Such crisis ghosts are not uncommon in our area; you may have experienced this ghostly guest yourself.

A Sisterly Specter in Rumson

According to an account provided by a long-time Rumson resident who we will call Linda, experienced a visit from a crisis ghost not so long ago. Linda and her twin sister, Louise, were inseparable ever since their birth. As was the custom in those days their mother dressed them in identical pink bonnets and play suits. Eventually it was sneakers, prom dresses and then wedding gowns.

Strangely, the girls never seemed to argue; they were always one another's very best friend. They shared a small pink and yellow bedroom, clothes, makeup, and once or twice boyfriends. Eventually they each married and came to live just two blocks from one another in the same local town.

Linda and Louise spoke several times each day, and visited every single day; even if it was just for a five-minute chat. Their children were more like brothers and sisters than cousins. Above all the two sisters trusted one another explicitly. They shared their inner most secrets, worries, and failures. Their hopes and dreams were a constant topic of conversation. They were such a pair that their teenage children laughingly called them the "pigeon sisters," after the characters in an episode of the Odd Couple.

One day Linda gave her sister the usual morning phone call. There was no answer. Although she thought it to be strange at the time, she considered that perhaps Louise was still in the shower. She waited half an hour and called again. There was still no answer. An uneasiness arose in Linda's chest, something wasn't right. She tried one more time, but the phone rang endlessly.

She dumped her coffee down the sink, grabbed her jacket and keys as she dashed out the door. Linda usually walked to Louise's house, but something was different about this morning. She jumped into her car and sped around the two blocks. She smiled to herself thinking how Louise would tease her about driving over instead of taking the four-minute walk.

When she pulled into the driveway, she saw that Linda's car was still in the garage. The door was locked, that was unusual. Linda tapped on the door and called out to her sister, 'Hey Lou, it's me," When she got no response she untangled Louise's house key from her key fob and opened the door.

That is when she found her. Louise was lying on the floor in a great heap as if she simply melted onto the floor. The next days became a blur; decisions were made, services were attended, and children comforted. They were the worst days she had ever known. Without her sister, Linda found it difficult to face each day. She often found herself feeling angry whenever she heard people laughing. As time passed Linda grew more and more depressed. She had difficulty carrying out daily tasks, and sometimes just being awake was just too painful.

One gray and rainy morning Linda sat up in bed drinking a cup of black coffee. She reached for the remote control for the TV and ended the mindless chatter on the morning talk shows. Her eyes came to rest on an old photo on her nightstand. It was the two of them, both pregnant at the time, posed in front of an old aluminum Christmas tree. As she smiled sadly at the photo the trickle of tears became a deluge. Her guttural sobs seemed to ricochet off the bedroom walls as she laid her head back against the pillow and closed her eyes.

As she opened her eyes she caught something move off the far right. She turned her head to gaze toward the bedroom door. For an instant, the world stood still; there is the doorway stood Louise. She appeared exactly like the last time Linda had seen her alive, in her jogging suit and sneakers. She looked at Linda and smiled lovingly.

Linda gasped and leapt from the bed with arms outstretched. Before she could reach the doorway, her sister held her hand up in the stop gesture. She never stopped smiling but slowly shook her head no, "No, not yet," she whispered. In the next instant, she disappeared.

This was the only time Louise ever came to visit Linda. Somehow

Louise knew that on that day, her sister desperately needed her comfort. Linda is still saddened by the loss of her sister. But now she understands; someday the twins will be united again.

Group 3: Residual Ghosts

The residual ghost is one of the most common paranormal events reported. This spirit lives out their last few hours of living on this earth, over and over again in an endless agony. It is like a great picture loop which repeats without end. These specters do not seem to have consciousness or intelligence; nor can they interact or alter their pattern. These sightings may be contemporary or be time slips where the environment is witnessed in the era of the apparition. An eighteenth century residual apparition may appear repeatedly, with full period attire, hair styles, mannerisms, décor, and even foods evident. Such hauntings may be traumatic in nature, or may be simply meaningful events from their life.

Closely related are mental imprints. This residual tends to focus on one particular event, accident, murder, execution or some traumatic scene. The incident itself is the apparition. These phenomena are accompanied by sounds such as footsteps, cries, moans, wails, creaks, and slamming of doors. They likely occur on very specific dates, and a precise time of day. Others occur during specific kinds of weather or are associated with a historic era such as a war, depression, or famine. As with other residuals these specters do not have consciousness and will not interact. In general, this form of apparition is believed to fade over time.

Another aspect of a residual is the tradition ghost. This is an earthbound spirit which remains at one location. This might be an historic building or location which was very important to that person in life. These hauntings go on for many years. They do not interact with humans and may be recognized as ancestors or others who have lived at that location. They appear solid and walk and act naturally, usually dressed in period attire. This is the kind of ghost likely to walk thru walls and doors, as often the remodeling of a structure is not perceived by the ghost of a different era.

The Scepter of Lizzie Farrow: Red Bank's Unsolved Murder

Residual sightings have been known for centuries here on the peninsula. One account dates back to the summer of 1892. The murder of a young Irish immigrant woman named Lizzie Farrow would spark one of the largest man hunts in Red Bank's history as well as one of the longest residual hauntings in the area.

After a day's work as a domestic in the Broad street home of the well-known Cornwall family of Red Bank, Lizzie met her friend Mary, and the two walked down Front Street to visit a mutual friend. It was around nine o'clock when they started back to their respective lodgings. They chatted as they walked up Maple until they came to Monmouth street. They parted here as Mary lived nearby, while Lizzie headed back to her boarding house on Bridge Avenue.

Lizzie was nearly home, just three doors away, when the killer struck. She was found lying in the street mumbling incoherently. A large bloody gash across the back of her skull spewed blood across the sidewalk. Despite their best of efforts, she slipped into unconsciousness and died.

The murder became the talk of the town. There was concern that the town had a serial attacker as just six months before another young woman had been attacked in a similar manner, in the same part of town. The culprit had not been caught. Although the first victim, Annie Van Winkle had survived the attack, her health continued to deteriorate and she died a few years later.

The massive manhunt for the killer resulted in multiple suspects. Several individuals were questioned at length and a few even jailed for a period of time. Formal murder charges were never filed, however, due to lack of evidence. A few weeks later the board of commissions held a debate to decide if the board should offer a reward for the capture of those responsible for the murders. The debate centered around the legality of the board to spend tax money on such an endeavor. As a result of the heated dispute, one of the board members, Mr. Drohan put up the reward money himself. Despite multiple tips and leads, and even a fraudulent claim from a man who also claimed to be attached, the crime went unsolved.

Soon after the funeral there were multiple claims of sightings of the murdered Lizzie. They all occurred in the vicinity of the train station on Bridge Avenue, and always very close to the boarding house where she had once lived. The descriptions of the apparition are identical. Lizzie strides anxiously down the street, with her head down, and her long skirt rustling softly against her legs. She pulls a faded cloak together with her left hand. As she nears her old boarding house she lurches forward, as if some heavy object had crashed against the base of her head. She loses her balance, collapsing to the pavement. She mumbles incoherently for a few seconds and then lies lifeless on the pavement.

The apparition was observed frequently for the next few years. It was always on a Thursday night on Bridge Avenue, and always near the train station. After a while the ghostly visits of Lizzie Farrow faded away. With it waned the memory of Lizzie Farrow's murder.

Apparition of a Traitor: A Phantom Stalks Navesink

Another residual haunting from the days of the Revolutionary War is well known here on the peninsula. This ghost, the specter of General Charles Lee, haunts the tip of the Highlands. Each night the specter moves back and forth between two different look out sites as if he can't decide which is the correct one to use. He uses a handheld telescope to scan the waters of the bay in search of something, or perhaps someone. He wears a dirty and disheveled Revolutionary War general's uniform which has been stripped of its buttons, insignias, and metals. He appears to be muttering or cursing, although no sound is ever heard.

Charles Lee, a former British military leader, moved to Virginia in 1773. When the revolution started, Lee resigned his commission in the British army and offered his services to the Continental Congress. With such extensive experience as commander, the patriots gladly accepted his offer. General Lee fully expected to be named commander and chief, a job which went to George Washington. Initially Lee refused to serve, when he didn't get the job, but then relented.

General Lee arrogantly demanded to know the rational for being denied the position. Congress obliged by informing him that there was some concern about his close relationship with the British army; and in addition, he was considered not be a gentleman. Lee was arrogant, crude and coarsely spoken, slovenly in appearance, and he expected to be paid upfront.

Lee quickly became known as an indecisive commander who frequently ignored direct orders, and made decisions not in the interest of the Patriot cause. On several occasions he slowed down troop movements when ordered to expedite, or retreated when told to advance. In addition, he maintained a constant stream of correspondence with the Continental Congress complaining about Washington. The matter came to a head when he failed to advance under a direct order from Washington at the Battle of Monmouth. Lee was stripped of command and eventually court martialed. His political connections within the Continental Congress resulted in the decision that there was insufficient evidence of condemn him to death. He retired to Virginia and died of a fever in Philadelphia in 1882.

Interestingly documents found in 1885 verified that Lee was indeed in collusion with the British, and while serving as a general in the Continental Army was indeed a spy and traitor. So, we can only assume that the apparition of General Charles Lee is spending his eternity pacing the hilltops of the Navesink Highlands, still waiting for his British comrades to rescue him.

Ghosts Who Cannot Cross Over

There are those who will say that all ghosts are those which have for some reason refused to, or are unable to cross over to the next dimension. There appears to be multiple reasons why this occurs.

Some spirits are afraid to move on. They don't seem to understand what has happened to them, and may be afraid of leaving what they know here on earth. Some seem to be trapped in their own fears and doubts. Still others may be under the influence of a negative spirit and are being prevented from walking to the light.

In some cases, it is said that spirits will not cross over if they die far from home. They wander the universe attempting to travel to their home before crossing over. Many of these have been wrenched away from life by violence, suicide, or a horrific event, and simply do not know where to go.

Another spirit who cannot cross over are those who do not realize they are dead. For whatever reason, they go on as if they are still alive. There is some debate whether this kind of ghost can see humans or not. It seems reasonable that they do, since the classic example of this kind of haunting occurs when an older person who has lived in a residence for many years passes away. Unfortunately, he or she does not realize they are dead and continue residing in the house as they did while alive. A new owner moves into the house and the ghost sees these humans as invaders. This can cause very stressful hauntings.

Ghost children often fall into this category as well. In general, ghost children have been wrenched from life before their time and don't understand where they are. They likely do not realize they are dead, and are confused by their environment. They are lonely little souls that may be trapped where they died. Death most likely was a horrific accident, terrifyingly violent, or a long painful illness. These lonely spirits tend to be exceptionally sad and needy, and often require help in crossing over.

Likewise, ghosts with unfinished business often fail to cross over. There is something they didn't finish before death or something so very important that they can or will not leave until the task is completed. In some cases, the spirit just wants to keep check on their family to insure they are OK, or a lover might stay around trying to help his beloved find a new love. Yet others, usually mothers, want to be there and help raise their child.

Other ghosts have less altruistic motives. A specter who was murdered or tortured, may seek vengeance on the person or family of person who was responsible. They can be difficult spirits to convince to cross over, as they are never really satisfied.

Ahchintak: Navarumsunk's Persistent Phantom

In one such case Ahchintak, a Lenape brave, has been unable to cross over for nearly a hundred and fifty years. He lived here on the peninsula with his tribe until 1755 when the government forced the Lenape into a deceitful land-for-nonviolence deal. It required the tribe to relocate to a settlement area in Burlington county. The settlement compelled the Indians to adapt to a European life style. The settlement under the direction of a Christian missionary, had houses similar to those of the settlers, a meeting hall and a gristmill. The settlement was such a failure that within a few years the tribe moved to upper New York state to join other native American tribes.

Ahchintak, however, would have none of that. He simply refused to leave his home on the Navarumsunk peninsula. He had carried the name Ahchintak with him even into adulthood, for his stubbornness was evident since childhood. He was not very sociable with his tribe and certainly not with any settlers he encountered. He lived alone with his wife, who bore the brunt of his dreadful temper.

It was not uncommon for him to defy the common decisions of the tribe so no one was surprised when he simply refused to leave with the tribe for Burlington County. He remained at the encampment with his wife and continued his antagonistic relationship with his settler neighbors.

Shortly after the tribe settled into the settlement they got word that Ahchintak was behaving aggressively towards the settlers on the peninsula. They feared that his behavior would endanger the non-violence agreement the tribe had established with the settlers. An emissary was sent to convince Ahchintak to join the tribe in the new settlement. He was never heard from again. When he failed to return, another messenger was sent. He too disappeared without a trace. Later Ahchintak boldly admitted he had killed them with his tomahawk for entering his property.

Shortly afterwards settlers tried to intervene when Ahchintak was caught beating his wife. When they rescued the bruised and bleeding woman she explained that she had merely suggested that she wanted to go live with the remainder of the tribe. That very night Ahchintak drowned his wife in a horse trough and left her body in the center of the settlers' village.

He remained on his tiny tract of land for some years until he died. In fact, it seems that he never left at all. Soon afterwards the apparition of the vengeful brave, bloody tomahawk in hand, was first seen roaming the paths and roads of the peninsula, searching for something, or perhaps someone. Accounts of the sighting have continued over the years, with occasional sights even today.

The ghost of Ahchintak is a force to be reckoned with. He is a towering muscular image in full native dress. He wears worn moccasins, deerskin leggings and a long deerskin tunic. A thin rawhide headband encircles his head from which two inverted feathers hang down his back. His face is set in an earnest search. His dark eyes dart back and forth as he searches for invisible enemies; or perhaps potential prey. His face is crunched into a scow and he breathes heavily spewing a low guttural growing sound.

It seems that Amchitka's need for revenge has prevented his spirit from crossing over to a more peaceful existence. This need for revenge seems to power this negative phantom, forcing him to remain in this sphere where his time has long since passed.

Group 5: Ghostly Objects and Animals

Those ghostly encounters associated with non-living and animals are a unique genre of spirits. Throughout the centuries history has recorded sightings of spiritually possessed (haunted) inanimate objects. This can be anything from a child's toy or doll, to a train or even a ship. It can be a mother's favorite photograph of her infant, or Grandfather's favorite shotgun. It may not be a rare or expensive item; it could something as inane as a cowboy hat, a favorite book, or even a broken clock.

Sometimes these objects take on characteristics of residuals and simply repeat a specific behavior over and over in a never-ending cycle. Such is the case of the Flying Dutchman, a phantom sailing ship, has been witnessed by thousands of mariners over the ages. The Dutchman sails endlessly, forever battling a gale, even in the calmest of seas

Other times the objects may behave more like intelligent spirits and appear to interact with the living. Some haunted objects resemble ghosts who have not been able to cross over, still others appear to be seeking revenge or be attempting to complete some unknown task. Some are capable of sound while others seem to lack consciousness.

This phenomenon is believed to arise when huge amounts of human emotion pass through the specific object. It seems that some objects are more likely than others to be haunted. Skulls, houses, buses, trains, jewelry, weapons, even televisions and computers have been known to be possessed by a spirit.

The small town of Urbana, Ohio has been a railroad town for more than a hundred years. It is one of the many small towns through which Abraham Lincoln's funeral train passed as the body of the assassinated president was taken from Washington to his home in Illinois for burial in the spring of 1865. Each April 29th, shortly after two am, the phantom funeral train, adorned with black bunting, rushes through the Urbana Station. The specter has continued for well over a hundred years.

Many authors conclude that often these possessed objects may be culturally sensitive. In Great Britain weapons and jewelry is most likely to be haunted, while in America toys and dolls are the most frequent objects. In some cultures it is special beads, prayer books, candles, or even trees or plants.

In cultures where animals are kept as pets, there is considerable discussion about the possibility of afterlife for these beloved animals. There is huge debate among folks who like to debate such things whether animals have souls or not.

An equal number of pet owners believe without a doubt that their beloved pet does have a soul and that they will be reunited with that pet in the afterlife. The literature is chocked full of accounts of apparitions, manifestations, and other paranormal evidence that beloved pets have lingered after death and have spiritually interacted with their masters.

The early Egyptians certainly attributed an afterlife to certain animals. It was not uncommon for a Pharaoh to be buried with his many earthly belongings which included wives, slaves, and pets. These were all sacrificed so that the souls could accompany the master into the next dimension.

Ghost investigators will confirm that they come across animal spirits frequently in their work. Sometimes they are family pets and other times they are animals associated with tragic events, or just a particular situation, or a specific time in history.

There are countless accounts of a beloved family pet who lingers after it has passed away. Owners report hearing a familiar whine, a bark, sniff, or the sound of toenails on a tile floor. Some have seen indentations in the pet's bed, or felt a cold nose on their forehead. Some pets have served as guardian angels or watched over their humans, growling or chasing away dangers. According to most reports these spirits stay a short while and then usually fade away.

These phantoms are found most frequently when the human and the animal spent long periods of time in stressful or dangerous situations. This is true of soldiers and their military dogs, policemen and their canines; not to mention those with seeing eye dogs or emotional support animals. An account shared by a long time Fair Haven resident testifies to this phenomenon.

Arnold's Daily Duty: A Fair Haven Phantom

Back in the days of the paddle wheelers the little village of Fair Haven woke early as the sound of the steam whistles echoed up and down the Navesink. Like a gust from a nor' easter the sound of the ship's airhorn ricocheted along the single lane streets that lay perpendicular to the river. The sound woke the village telling them another day had begun. For Arnold, it was the signal that it was time to get to work.

For Arnold had many responsibilities. One of his many tasks was to greet the steamships when they docked in Fair Haven. He could hear the ship coming while it was still up river, and always managed to be waiting at the pier when she docked. He waited patiently to see who alighted from the boats, and watched apprehensively as locals strolled up the gangways for their daily trip into the city. After the ship departed Arnold trotted back to DeNormandie Avenue and resumes his usual routine.

Arnold spent the rest of the morning visiting his neighbors on the street, one after another. He checked to see who was cooking, or cleaning, or getting ready for work. He wandered across lawns, checked out new flower beds, and was sitting beneath the forsythia in time to watch the children meander up the street toward the school.

Usually someone offered him a morning snack, and if he played his cards right there would be lunch farther down the lane. And always there was a treat here and there whenever he showed up. When school let out Arnold was there on his post greeting the kids with a wagging tail, and jostling with them as they ran home to change into their play clothes. Yes, Arnold was a dog.

He officially lived on De Normandie Avenue, but considered the adjacent streets his territory as well. He deemed the families on the street as his family, and the kids on the street as his kids. In addition to meeting the steamboats, Arnold also kept watch over the children on the street. A crying baby or the wail of a youngster with skinned knee brought Arnold running. He also kept a close eye on strangers on the street. Whenever the kids went exploring or went down to the river, Arnold went too. Sometimes he just sat on the little sandy beach area and watched, other times he joined in the fun and came home just like the kids, soaked to the skin and covered in sand.

Everyone agreed that Arnold was a handsome rascal. He was part Labrador Retriever and part who knows what. His coat was a rich fawn color with spurts of white around his face, on his chest, and paws. Yet his ear tips were almost a copper color. As Arnold grew older the white hair around his muzzle intensified and the tips of his ears too took on a whiteish hue

That spring people noticed that Arnold, who was now called Old Arnold, had slowed down. He no longer raced across lawns to meet the steamboats, but rather trotted at a leisurely pace in a rather nonchalant manner. He maintained his daily rounds, but was less likely to visit the entire street before noon. He was often seen sleeping beneath the forsythia bush or stretched out on one of Mrs. Smith's chase longue chairs. He still tried to keep up with the kids, but it was more difficult now, and so usually Arnold would just sit and watch the fun instead of joining his favorite game of keep away.

Then one morning Arnold could not be found. No one met the steamboat that morning, and there was no one to watch the children as they headed up the street to school. They found him later, lying beneath the forsythia bush. Arnold had passed away.

There was much sadness on the street for several days. Everyone talked about what a wonderful dog Arnold had been. His master buried him there beneath the forsythia because it was his favorite place. At first children brought bouquets of dandelion flowers for his grave; but then the grass grew over his plot and by the time summer arrived people had stopped talking about Arnold altogether.

The Fourth of July was on a Saturday that year, and the entire town geared up for a busy and exciting weekend. There would be boat rides, fishing, swimming, picnics, and back yard clam bakes. On the eve of the holiday the temperatures soared into the high 90's. Windows were opened wide, kids ran about in their swim suits, and the older folks tried to keep cool by sitting under shade trees with a cool drink.

By midafternoon most of the children were down at the river. Some waded at the water's edge, others splashed one another in water up to their waists. Three or four boys tossed a ball back and forth over an imaginary net. A few older kids were holding a swimming tournament, swimming laps between the shore and the outer boundary of the swim area which was marked by a single white rope.

Several mothers sat on the sand chatting with one another. They periodically scanned the water watching the kids at play. The women had just got into a discussion of the best recipes for chowder when they noticed a commotion in the water several yards from shore. The children were all shouting and screaming, pointing toward the far side of the beach.

The women soon joined in the screaming, for there in the deeper water, away from all the other swimmers, a small child in a reddish orange swimsuit was flailing in the water. Little arms waved frantically in the air, and then suddenly disappeared. On woman raised her skirt to her knees and rushed into the water. But she soon stumbled and fell into the water herself.

Suddenly a large fawn colored dog darted across the beach and dove into the water. It paddled to the site where the child had disappeared. For a moment, no one could see the dog; just then his head emerged from the water. In his teeth, he clutched the reddish orange swim suit. He started swimming toward shore with the small child dangling from his mouth. When he reached the beach, he dropped the child at the feet of the women.

Help seemed to come from everywhere and soon the child was being whisked away. Everyone stood about chattering excitedly about what had

just happened. It was several minutes before anyone th<
the dog who had rescued the child. It was nowhere to b
claimed to be his master, and no one remembered havin
the neighborhood.

The adults were in quandary about the identification of the dog. One
person said it was wearing a collar, but another one held it was definitely
not wearing a collar. On person declared that it was a fawn colored dog
while someone else supposed it was more of a whitish tan. An older boy
insisted that it was probably a lab, or maybe just a mutt. One man said that
it had reddish ears. But that didn't help, no one could remember having
ever seen the dog before.

Then a small voice broke through the chatter, "I know who the dog is!"
he announced, "It's Old Arnold, I'd know him anywhere." A few grownups
laughed out loud at the child. Everyone knew that Old Arnold was dead.
He had been gone several months. Some smiled and patted the boy on his
back, others looked away, or exchanged bewildered glances.

Later that night as folks settled down for the night, they began to re-
play the day's events and consider the possibility the child had suggested.
Eventually most came to agree; it could have been none other than Old
Arnold who came back from the grave to save one his kids.

Group 6: Living Ghosts and Photographic Specters

This unusual genre of specters is also one of the most interesting. This
manifestation occurs when the soul has left the body but the individual is
still alive. This can occur when an individual is very near death, and the
spirit leaves to say goodbye to a loved one.

But we usually associate the term with the projection of a living person,
an identical copy seen by others, or sometimes by the individual himself. It
may be the person at his true age, or even an earlier age. In some instances
the projection of ourselves, and is such that others see it and you don't.
These ghosts show both intelligence and self-awareness.

In this instance, someone may claim to have seen you at a specific
location at a very specific time. But you know you were nowhere near the

⌐. The image is so perfect that they will likely argue with you about the appearance.

Occasionally individuals see their own image, this is known as a doppelgänger. This is word taken from the German, *dopple* means double, and *ganger* means walker or doer. Many claim it foretells death. It is said that Abraham Lincoln saw his doppleganger in a mirror on the morning in which he was assassinated.

Another peculiar ghost is the photographic ghost. This spirit is not observed at the moment the photo is taken. Yet once the photo is completed the apparition is clearly visible. Sometimes it is just a cloudlike form, other times it is a full body, identifiable manifestation.

One Last Visit to Nana's House

A few years ago, a man from Little Silver recounted his adventure with such a photographic ghost. For as long as Matthew could remember he had spent his summers at the Jersey shore. Long before he was born his grandparents had purchased a rambling house just off Ocean Avenue in Monmouth Beach. The house was full of memories of carefree summer days; splashing in the ocean and digging clams along the river.

Most of all he remembered Nana. He recalled her clam bakes out in the back yard, of being washed down with the garden hose when he came back from the beach, and even of Nana's elegant Christmas eve dinners where he often complained about the mandatory shirt and tie.

The house was full of memories of Nana. They had moved to the beach permanently when Grandpa retired. And even after he died, Nana stayed. She always claimed it was her one true home, and she declared that she would never leave it. But Nana was gone now, and it was time to put the house on the market.

Most of the family had scattered across the country except for Matthew who settled down in nearby Little Silver. It became his task to organize the distribution of her belongings. He decided to hold one last family reunion in the old house, even planned one of Nanas elegant dinners to say goodbye.

On the appointed weekend, despite the cold weather, they all came back for one last weekend at the beach. Soon the house was filled with laughter and the clink of wine glasses. The long dining table was set with Nana's best china, silverware, and linens. There was a fire roaring in the hearth and on the mantel, was a large framed photograph of the entire family, taken two years ago, on Nana's ninetieth birthday. They all stood together, in their best attire (shirts and ties, of course) with Nana settled regally in the very center in her favorite wingback chair.

Everyone was in a fine mood, chatting and laughing, and sharing the latest family news with one another. Soon they were recounting stories from their days here at the beach. The subject always came back to Nana, and her firm but loving manner. Nana was indeed a woman to be reckoned with. She was the matriarch of the family, she knew it, and lived accordingly. They laughed about the times they might try to tell Nana a fib, and how it was never successful. They chuckled over the great debates they used to have about planning an event, knowing it was Nana who made the final decision.

They finished dinner, and were waiting the forty-five minutes which Nana always insisted must pass before dessert would be served. Matthew pulled out his camera and suggested they have one last family photo taken in the old house. There were a couple of good natured snipes about Matthew and his love of photography, but everyone agreed it was a good idea.

While the family jockeyed for positon in front of the fireplace Matthew set up the tripod and double checked his remote control. Everyone was here for this one last photo; everyone except Nana. It took several attempts as people laughed at the wrong time, or one of the toddlers wandered away. Finally, the camera clicked, and someone shouted, "It's a take!" The family scurried back to their spots on the sofas and chairs which surrounded the great hearth.

When Matthew checked the images, he couldn't believe his eyes. There in the photograph was the family smiling back at the camera. In the center, exactly in the center of the photograph, was Nana regally posed in her favorite wing back chair. It was a full body apparition, somewhat grayish in color. Obviously, Nana was not about to miss this last family photograph.

For as long as such records have been kept the two rivers region has been blessed or cursed (you choose the word) with countless ghostly and supernatural encounters. These descriptions are just a few of the accounts of the apparitions, specters, and the singularly peculiar events which occurred and continue to occur here, in the land between the two rivers.

The Ghostly Spirit of Mary & Me: A Tale of Prohibition

On January 17,1920, the news flashed across the nation as countless headlines proclaimed the beginning of Prohibition in the United States. On that very day, the 18th amendment to the Constitution went into effect. Known as the Volstead Act, it forbid the manufacture, sale or transport of intoxicating liquors within the United States. The Act did not forbid the consumption of the alcohol, but rather forbid its production and distribution by both private and commercial means. But it had the same effect. This was the first day of what was to become thirteen years of civil disobedience and internal turmoil across the nation. It came complete with moonshine stills, clandestine breweries, bootlegging, fraudulent medical practices, smuggling, hidden speakeasys, corruption, and even murder. To many locals of the Jersey shore it was more like a second civil war.

Prohibition did not happen overnight, nor was it the first attempt to control what some considered a nationwide scrounge of drunkenness. The excessive consumption of alcohol in America had been the topic of many editorials in both this country and Europe. Americans were reputed to be serious "boozers."

The controversy, which was intertwined with the suffrage movement for a time, had been going on for almost a hundred years. The intense ruthless campaigning by temperance groups combined with considerable political "wheeling and dealing" finally was successful. The Act became law over the veto of President Woodrow Wilson in January, 1919. A year later the Act went into effect under a flurry of last minute hoarding and large scale procurements of alcohol before the midnight deadline.

Newspaper headlines across the globe flashed the news that America had gone dry. At the stroke of midnight when the Act went into effect both private and commercial stills immediately went into production. Across America in kitchens and basements of private homes, in clandestine warehouses, and camouflaged factories, the underground distillation of spirits commenced in earnest.

The AMA immediately sought out a special exclusion to the Volstead Act citing the need for the use of alcohol in certain medicines. Soon the medicinal market was flooded with various health tonics and remedies containing alcohol. As these required a prescription, Americans began seeing their physicians more frequently seeking these tonics to "promote and maintain" their health. Not to miss out on the opportunity, several contemporary American drug store chains credit their tremendous growth to their sales of these health tonics during Prohibition.

Wine makers and other brewers contrived to continue their operations despite the new law. Some operated liquor stores masquerading as ice cream parlors, candy stores, or tea rooms. Most brewers sold malt syrup which could easily be made into beer. Wine makers sold a grape brick which if properly processed could be made into wine. Even a .5 % alcohol beverage known as "Near Beer" gained popularity.

Among the best known in our area is Laird's Apple Jack, which has been in business since 1698. During Prohibition, Lairds survived by selling an assortment of apple products until it attained a federal permit to produce a medicinal apple brandy.

While the effect of Prohibition nationwide was significant, the effect on the day to day life of local shore residents was tumultuous. Practically overnight, bootlegging in the form of "rum running' became a local, and sometimes a community industry. Since the legislation was not particularly popular in the area to begin with, it took little encouragement to persuade locals to participate in the budding rum running business. Both professional and recreational fishermen, and frankly anyone with a boat promptly became one of the well know "rum runners" of the Jersey shore.

This form of bootlegging sprung up all along the New Jersey coast. Yet it was here on the Eastern Monmouth County shoreline, and along the banks of our twin rivers, the Navesink and Shrewsbury that rum running became an enormous, although illegal industry. The ragged coastline, with its many modest inlets, secluded coves, and winding creeks was an asset to the local bootleggers. Access to the ocean enabled smugglers to operate with relative ease, and our proximity to the dense populations of New York, Philadelphia, Washington, and Baltimore provided the market. It is said that one could easily deduce when a fisherman began running rum because his family started to eat better, and his bills got paid.

Regulating the Act was under the control of the Internal Revenue Service. To police the Act the government called upon the newly formed Coast Guard. (The Life Saving Service was combined with the Revenue Cutter Service to create the Coast Guard in 1915) This conversion into a police force did not go well with many in the life saving units or the newly formed Coast Guard as they were frequently neighbors and relatives of the local rum runners.

In addition, the passage of the 16th amendment, just seven years earlier, had levied a permanent and restrictive federal income tax on all individual income. This not only did not endear the locals to the Internal Revenue Service, but also made it the butt of many jokes, satire, and earnest attempts to avoid paying the tax all together.

The term "rum runner" originated from previous smuggling operations. For many years Caribbean rum manufactures smuggled rum onto the Florida shore using a caravan of small boats to avoid tariffs and taxes. The process was the same. Smaller boats, usually anything with a flat bottom that would hold a good amount of cargo, and having a fast engine, was the perfect boat for this job. For local workers, making a meager income at the beginning of the 1920's, it was a chance of a lifetime.

Originally the US territorial limit from the coast was three nautical miles. It was just beyond this site that the famous "rum row" formed. Dozens of large freighters stocked with liquor from Europe, Canada, Bermuda and the Caribbean jockeyed for position. As the ships were in international waters the government was unable to prevent the flotilla of ships from anchoring. These large ships called mother ships, remained in place for months at a time, serving as floating warehouses. Freighters from around the world supplied the mother ships daily with renewed cargo of whiskey, scotch, gin, vodka, bourbon, and rye. When the sun set, the fleet of local rum runners raced to the mother ships and off loaded the precious cargo.

For the hometown rum runner, often referred to as "rummers" by locals, it was a quick trip out to the awaiting freighters. Under the cover of darkness and with a bit of luck, they quickly loaded their small crafts and raced for the shore to a designated meeting spot somewhere along the ragged coast, or at a secluded dock on one of our two sister rivers. Here they could offload their cargo and collect their fee. Even a small boat could make the equivalent in today's money of one hundred and fifty dollars per trip. A rummer could make two a night if he were lucky. Sources say 35,000 cases of liquor were smuggled each night along our local shore.

Many of the rummers were revealed to be true entrepreneurs. These boatmen didn't approach the freighter empty handed. They came with groceries, vegetables, mail, baked goods, warm clothing, newspapers, and even fresh water. They sold these to the crew members of the mother ships and often carried messages and mail back to the mainland.

As soon as the rummers tied their small craft alongside the mother ships their cargo was whisked onto the mother ship while the contraband alcohol was loaded into the boats. The delivery might be in barrels, casks, boxes, burlap bags, and the famous McCoy's "hams." Rummers knew that if the Coast Guard pursued them their only alternative was to toss the valuable alcohol overboard. A smuggler named McCoy devised a clever packaging for the liquor. Called a ham, it was a burlap bag in which bottles of booze were tied together, and then enclosed in a layer of salt. If the rummer was being pursued, he tossed his "hams" overboard into relatively shallow water. In a few days, the salt dissolved and the bottles began to float. The rummer could swing back and retrieve the goods.

When the government moved the territorial limit to 12 miles the mother ships simply raised anchor and moved out 13 miles from shore. World War I had just ended and there was ample army surplus of aircraft and tank engines which the rum runners bought inexpensively and installed in their boats. This made them high powered and faster than the revenuers.

The entire thing made for rather delicate community relations as many coast guard members lived next door to school mates or even relatives who were running rum. In general people looked the other way. Several boat yards and docks in our area did take sides, refusing the Coast Guard access to dock or to refuel.

Locals tried to camouflage their boats, painting each side different colors, adding or removing fishing gear, or even repainting the nameplate on the stern daily with a different name. It was serious business for the rummer. If he were caught by the Coast Guard both the cargo and the boat were confiscated. Many of the faster boats captured by the Coast Guard were rechristened and used as chase boats. If the boat was not suitable for Coast Guard use, the former owner could only stand by and watch as his boat was burned.

It wasn't long before organized crime realized the tremendous profits involved in smuggling and began to take over the business. Now the local runners had two foes. They not only had to worry about the federal agents, but now faced a band of gangsters equipped with both high-speed boats and heavy duty arms. When a rum war broke out between the crime families, the local rum runners were caught in the middle. Soon a legion of gangsters focused on driving the locals out of the rum running business.

Organized criminals attacked local rummers, killed crews, burned crafts, and terrorized families and friends. Their tactics involved collusion, sabotage, and murder. Their corruption of local leaders was blatant and actual warfare broke out on local waters and along the shoreline.

Within a few years rum running was totally a mob business. Long before the stock market crashed in 1929 bootlegging was firmly in the hands of organized crime. Not only did this eliminate the competition of rum running from local rivermen, but resulted in the pervasive mob violence spilling out onto local streets in places like Long Branch, Oceanport, Sea Bright, Red Bank, and Atlantic Highlands. Anxiety over the bloodshed spread not only among residents but among visitors as well. Almost immediately the vacation industry died along the northern shore.

As tourism dried up in the Two Rivers region, so did countless related jobs, creating long lines of the unemployed. Long before the government gave depression its name, working people knew the nation was in trouble. Just as inland folks lived off the land as best they could, planting gardens anywhere crops would grow, so too the rivermen and coastal fishermen lived off the local waters. Fishing, crabbing, eeling, and clamming were for some the only means of putting food on the table.

As is often the case, hard times aroused a series of peculiar, unexplainable, and even paranormal events. This is most assuredly true of the thirteen turbulent years of the Prohibition. The folklore of the area during Prohibition is bursting with accounts of strange apparitions, unexplained phenomena, and just plain creepy happenings.

One such tale takes place in the backwaters of the Shrewsbury River where the estuary begins to widen into an almost lake like appearance. Here the irregular coast line is dotted with an assortment of small coves, creeks, inlets and countless tidal pools. All along the shoreline, hidden among the seagrass and Phragmities, small docks cling onto the marsh.

Jessie had lived on the Shrewsbury his whole life. Just like his father before him, he was a fisherman. He worked the rivers and bay ten and twelve hours a day fishing and clamming, trying to feed his growing family. He lived with his wife and three children in a small ramshackle cottage in the small fishing community which was once known as Galilee.

Jessie had lived on the water for as long as he could remember. He had learned to swim before he could walk, and knew the names of every marine plant and animal found along the Jersey shoreline. He always knew he would become a fisherman long before he bought his first boat, the Mary & Me. He not only understood the tide cycle as well as he knew his own name, but could also identify the exact location of the Shrewsbury's many the hidden shoals which might endanger his boat. He knew the best clamming spots and had his own favorite fishing grounds both in the rivers and the nearby ocean.

When Prohibition was young he quickly realized he could supplement his meager income by doing a bit of rum running. It wasn't complicated. Each night after dark he and the Mary & Me simply motored down the Shrewsbury along the barrier island. He proceeded past the mouth of the

Navesink where the two rivers meet. From there it was a short run to the bay. After skirting Sandy Hook, he would race out to meet a freighter on rum row. He quickly picked up his cargo of illegal liquor, and retraced his path; rapidly and as unobtrusively as possible. He delivered his cargo to a designated dock on the Shrewsbury and was soon home, safe and sound.

Those times were good for Jess and his family. He put food on the table, the kids no longer wore hand me downs, and the worried look on his wife's face vanished. Although he never said it aloud, Prohibition was the best thing that ever happened to him.

Then gangsters from the organized crime families began taking over the rum running business. It quickly became a dangerous endeavor. Two of his friends had been murdered, and at least three fellow fishermen had simply disappeared during recent rum runs. He and the Mary& Me had been chased, and even shot at once. But after that last night on the river, the night he abandoned the Mary & Me, and just seconds before she exploded into a fiery ball of flames, Jessie gave up bootlegging for good.

With the loss of his boat and the serious injuries he sustained from the incident Jessie once again faced a meager existence. Once again, he knew the feeling of want, and fear he could not provide for his family. In the coming days and weeks Jessie's body healed, as much as it ever would. He walked with a limp now from the fractures and burns he suffered that night. Weakness in his legs and back prevented him from fishing anymore, so he began knitting nets for the other fishermen and made just enough to keep food on the table.

It was a particularly cool autumn night, ten long years later. Jessie limped across the small plank platform that served as a porch. Using his cane to support his weigh, he eased himself onto the top step and leaned against the worn four by four being used as a porch post. He looked up at the ceiling of the plywood roof and saw daylight. He sighed, and shook his head. He sat for a long time staring out across the river. He reached for his pipe and then remembered that he had no tobacco. He exhaled and shoved the pipe back into his windbreaker. There had been no tobacco for a very long time.

As he so often did, Jessie began thinking about the Mary & Me, and tried to remember when he first saw the apparition. He had witnessed the specter for so many years now. But it was no use, he couldn't remember the first time. Others had seen it before him, and it became the local chinwag for a while. Even his wife saw it before he did. One day years ago, Mary had charged into the cottage shrieking nonsensibly. She had seen the apparition of the Mary & Me, fully engulfed in flames floating towards the shore right in front of their house. Sometime later Jessie began to see it too. At first only once in a while, when the weather was cold and overcast like it was on that last night. Then it began to appear more and more often.

It was always the same. He saw his beloved Mary & Me floating aimlessly down the Shrewsbury, the pilothouse surround by huge flames. As he watched, she began curving toward the shore. There was a moment when she seemed to stop dead in the water. Then a loud boom echoed across the river as the sky filled with millions of fiery fragments of the Mary & Me. Although he would feel the heat from the explosion, his body stayed icy cold.

Now, he saw it often, always at night, regardless of the weather. It always seemed to appear when the household kitty was nearly empty, but then that was most of the time these days.

It had been his first real fishing boat, and he loved Mary & Me almost as much as he loved Mary, his wife. Local rumormongers and tattlers claimed the apparition was an evil omen. Although it broke his heart each time he watched her explode into millions of pieces, he began to look forward to the apparition. For some inexplicable reason, it reassured him of something he couldn't quite explain. And each and every time, he relived that final and unforgettable night.

Jessie sat on the steps until darkness spread across the river like an endless black shroud. Before his eyes the Mary and Me emerged from the marsh, fully ablaze. In an instant he was taken back to that night.

It was a cold windy day. The sky was overcast and bad weather threatened. The river was a muddy brown, swirling away from the tide which shoved the Phragmites against the shoreline. Along the sandy berm, the marsh gave way to a layer of packed snow.

Jessie shouted goodbye as he slammed the front door against the icy wind with one hand and balanced the basket of fresh baked bread and cakes with the other. He hurried toward the Mary & Me which sat gently rocking at the dock. Although it wasn't far to the river, the wind was so bitter that he pulled his ear flaps down around his head as he walked.

When he reached the Mary & Me he smiled, he couldn't help himself. She was a beautiful craft, perhaps not to others, but Jessie thought her to be beautiful. She was a worthy vessel with a small pilot house, and a deep flat floor that had carried many a full load of fish over the years. These days she was also doing a regular night time run, the rum run. But she didn't seem to mind the extra work. She had survived many a nor'easter, a few chases by the coast guard, and even one or two tussles with the gangsters.

As he prepared for the nightly run he remembered how shinny and white she used to look. Now that he was running rum he was forced to paint her different colors every few weeks in hopes of camouflaging her from the Coast Guard. Even her name plate had been switched many times. Coral Lady, Sweet Surprise, and Fish's Foe, were only a few of the names she had sported across her stern. But to Jessie she was always the Mary & Me.

By early evening he had collected and packed his "trading items" into baskets and carefully tucked them into the pilot house. In addition to the fresh baked goods complements of Mary, he had newspapers, tobacco, some vegetables, and several cans of coffee. He hastily wrote a price on the outside of the basket. He would sell these to the foreman on the freighter for a bit extra cash. He liked to call that his private stash, he used it to buy treats for his kids and always a little something for Mary.

It had started out like any other run. He always left the dock well after dark, and always with a full load of fuel. He headed along the Shrewsbury, looking like all the other boats on the way out for a night of fishing off the coast. He watched the lights in Sea Bright glistening off his starboard and soon caught a glimpse of the Highlands lights ahead to port. Soon he was in the bay moving toward the tip of Sandy Hook. The water was a bit choppier here than it had been in the river. But Jessie didn't mind, he focused on the course ahead. He wasn't alone on the water tonight, there seemed to be an armada of fisherman headed out to the deep water.

Jessie kept as close to the Hook as he dared. Once passed the tip he headed East-Southeast, hoping to avoid confrontation with either the Coast Guard or the gangsters. It added some time to the trip, but it was safer that way. As he navigated into the darkness Jessie checked his compass repeatedly. In the distance, he could make out a thin row of lights.

Jessie shivered and adjusted the woolen hat farther down on his head. Despite the bitter cold on the open ocean Jessie was in good spirits. After this run he would take a few days off to do some repair work on the cottage and spend time with Mary and the kids.

The ocean was relatively calm and there seemed to be little traffic on the route. He saw only a few other boats heading his direction. To anyone else they looked like regular fishermen, but Jessie knew them to be fellow rummers. As he approached the territorial limits he could see the mother ship, the giant freighter loaded with illegal liquor, bobbing gentling in the waves.

He checked his compass and chart once more, making certain he was safely within international waters before he turned on his running lights. Using a small lantern he flashed the signal to the freighter. For a few moments there was no response. Then he saw it, the quick double flash from the mother ship. It was safe to proceed.

As he approached he wondered what it was like to be aboard the mother ship for weeks and months at time, with no news, no mail, no Mary or the kids. As he pulled aside giant ropes fell from the deck which Jessie quickly attached to the both the bow and the stern of his boat.

The crew foreman peered down from above. Jessie immediately held up his large basket as high as he could. "Good man!" came the reply from the deck. Another long rope immediately dropped into the boat. Jessie quickly attached the basket to the line and in one quick motion the basket was hoisted onto the freighter.

At the same time two crewmen from the freighter scampered down a rope ladder and joined him on the deck of the Mary & Me. An enormous wench on the stern of the freighter whirled into action extending a long steel arm over the side of the freighter just above Jessie's boat. Attached to the steel cable was a hefty cargo net filled with dozens of barrels of Irish whiskey. As soon as it was within reach the two-man crew began hoisting the barrels aboard the Mary & Me. Jessie directed the loading to ensure that it would not shift during the trip back up river. When the net was empty, a crewman flashed a signal and the net was whisked back aboard the freighter. Jessie and crewmen quickly shook hands and wished one another luck. By the time the crewmen had reached the top of the rope ladder, Jessie had unleashed himself from the mother ship.

He checked to be certain his lights were doused and pulled away from the freighter. He eased away into the darkness, slowly at first as not to call any attention to himself. He checked his watch and realized he would be fighting the tide going home. That meant he couldn't travel as quickly as he would like, and with a full load he would burn a lot more fuel.

When he was some distance away he pushed the throttle forward and began the long dark journey. Jessie was fully alert now, for this was the dangerous segment of the trip. In addition to the difficulty of navigating totally in the dark, he also had to keep a keen eye out for both the Coast Guard and the gangsters. If the Coast Guard caught him they would arrest him, confiscate the cargo, and worst of all seize or destroy the Mary & Me. Confronting the gangsters could prove be even worse. They often traveled in packs, like wolves, and played by their own rules. They had no hesitation in robbing and killing anyone who they caught running rum.

The Mary & Me moved quickly but fervently towards the Highlands and the mouth of the Two Rivers. The air was frigid and the ocean a bit choppier, but Jessie paid little attention. He was focused on his path through the dark waters while constantly scanning the surface on each side of him. His eyes strained to peer through the darkness in search of both the light-colored hulls of the Coast Guard and the dark shadowy vessels more likely to be the gangsters.

He breathed uneasily, darting his eyes to and fro searching as far as the horizon in every direction. As he neared the tip of Sandy Hook he paused the boat dead in water for a moment to take a closer look at his surroundings. The route looked clear, Jess thrust the level forward and the Mary & Me darted passed the Hook and into the bay. He didn't slow down, not even as he approached the mouth of the rivers.

Just as he passed under the Highlands Bridge he saw something out of the corner of his eye. It was something small and dark on his starboard side. He turned to look again, it was definitely moving. The hair on the back of his neck stood straight up. He strained his eyes to scour the darkness, it was a boat and it was following him. The Mary and Me raced up the river. Jess checked the instrument panel and winced, if only he wasn't fighting the tide. He just couldn't make the speed he wanted.

As he approached the small sedge islands at the mouth of the Navesink he considered darting into the estuary and hiding among the scrub and reed beds. He thought better of it, he had to keep moving and try to disappear within the marshy cluster of islands in the Shrewsbury. Perhaps the Shrewsbury would be too shallow during this tide for the pursuit vessel. It was a treacherous run and Jess knew it. He had to keep an eye on the dark vessel pursing him and at the same time be careful to avoid the countless shoals and small sedge islands that dotted the Shrewsbury.

The boat was in high gear, pushing back against the current. The Mary & Me had never reached this speed before. At times, she seemed to be lifting right out of the water. Jessie frowned hearing a low moaning coming from the engine. Again, and again he looked at the vessel approaching him on his starboard. Each time he looked back he saw it was it was getting closer and closer.

Suddenly he heard another engine. For a second he thought it came from the Mary & Me. But it was not the Mary & Me, and it was loud and close, too close to be coming from the boat in pursuit. This time Jessie spun to look to port and gasped in horror. There, just few yards off his stern a black hulled speed boat was closed in on him. There were two of them! To his horror, Jessie saw three men aboard holding torches. He knew immediately what that meant. Although he was freezing cold sweat ran down his face.

Jessie tried to swerve back and forth to prevent from being over taken. But it was no use. There was a gun shot, and then the dark vessel pulled aside. In an instant, a burning torch flew through the air and handed on the bow of the Mary & Me.

Jessie saw the flames leaping towards the pilot house. They would reach the cargo of whiskey within minutes. He couldn't leave the wheel to fight the fire, yet he knew that at any moment all that alcohol would explode. He looked towards the shore and gave the wheel a hard right. The boat curved toward the marshland ahead. Jessie crawled over the barrels of whiskey to the stern. He crept up on the washboard and without pausing to glance back dove into the frigid water. Just then a huge fire ball filled in the night sky over the Shrewsbury. Millions of pieces of the Mary & Me fluttered down onto the water's surface. Within seconds a dark hulled speed boat was racing back downstream.

Jessie didn't remember hitting the water, or the initial searing burn from the explosion. He dove as deeply as he could, surfacing a several yards away. When he came up for air, he sputtered and gasped in the bitterly cold. His eyes failed to focus and he could see only a fiery glow against the night sky. He realized his beloved boat was gone before he knew he was seriously injured. Just then the searing pain hit him and for a moment he sank beneath the water.

He couldn't remember how he managed to get to shore. The most he could recall was swimming, well trying to swim. His left leg just would not move, and there was a penetrating kind of pain that took his breath away. Somehow, he found himself on the berm of a soggy patch of marsh.

Jessie didn't know how long he had laid there, but when he awoke it was daylight. He was covered with painful cuts and bruises, but nothing compared to unyielding pain in his leg. He tried to sit up but flopped back on the sand. When he finally managed to get a look at his leg all he could see as a bloody mass of charred skin and a ragged bone protruding from his pant leg.

To this day, Jessie still wonders how a neighbor had known to come over to the far side of the marsh to look for him; it was out of the way for sure. It really didn't matter; he was rescued and taken ashore. There he would spend many painful months recovering from his broken bones and burned flesh.

Jessie rubbed the tender skin of his leg and used the cane to lift the weakened leg onto the step. As he looked out over the river the wind picked up. At first it was just a waft air but then it became a steady wind. He felt the gust slap his face, and he smiled. She was coming again, he knew it. That was unusual, he had never seen the apparition twice in one night.

As he looked across the marsh a flicker of light appeared. Ever so slowly the glow grew brighter until the manifestation of the ship, fully engulfed in flames, drifted towards the shore. Jessie didn't turn his eyes away as the burning specter approached. All he saw was the Mary & Me as she used to be, her shining white hull and polished wooden trim glistening on an ocean of blue. Jessie's smile grew into a broad grin. She was so beautiful. She had fed his family for many years and had always brought him safely home. Even on that last night she had given it her all to bring him home.

It had been some time since Jessie has spoken of the apparition. For years, he had refused to discuss it, even with his wife, Mary. Locals who claimed to have seen it had been rebuffed when they tried to share their sightings.

It was not until the old man died that night, sitting on his porch steps, that the apparition vanished, and was never seen again.

Conundrum at
Loggy Hole Farm

Situated along the wetlands of the Shrewsbury River, extending along the Sycamore Avenue section of modern day Shrewsbury and Little Silver lies a 112-acre plot of land once known as Loggy Hole Farm. The farm no longer exists, replaced long ago by housing developments and businesses. Yet, as early as 1838 the property had already gleaned its curious name, as well as rumors of peculiar happenings on the property.

Although the farm exchanged hands several times over the years, its multiple owners retained the name Loggy Hole Farm well into the twentieth century. It was only after it was sold in 1925 by William Fanshawe, a prominent Shrewsbury and Manhattan land owner, that use of the name disappeared from the records.

Other than a few word of mouth stories, there is limited documentation of paranormal activity on the farm during the previous century and the early 1800's. The area remained sparsely populated, with land usage being primarily agricultural. But in 1838 the farm began a century long encounter with series of bizarre and inexplicable events.

Admittedly, landowners and especially farmers have been known to be particularly unconventional when naming their properties. Many simply use the family surname, while others employed humor or even sarcasm when giving title to their homesteads. Names like Rusty Fence Farm, Aikens Back Acres, or Spotted Ass Farm are typical of the more creative names given to personal homesteads. Yet over the years, many have questioned the reason for the use of such an obscure name for the farm as Loggy Hole.

We know that Loggy Hole Farm was well-known and successful throughout the years despite both its unattractive name, and the growing number of reported peculiar events happening there. The property, once part of Robert Allen's vast holdings was purchased by George Hance. He in turn left it to George Hance Patterson. It was during this time the number of inexplicable events increased significantly.

By 1892 Loggy Hole Farm had been sold once again. This time the farm belonged to E.C. Hazard, a New York business man who owned both a wholesale food distribution company as well as well a recently acquired tomato canning business, also located in Shrewsbury. Within a few short years Loggy Hole Farm became the center of his large vegetable canning business. By the 1890's Shrewsbury Ketchup was a popular condiment found on tables across the region. E.C. Hazard is equally well known for his insistence of purity and quality in food canning and was instrumental in passing the Pure Food and Drug Act in 1906.

After Hazard died the property was broken up and the farm sold to William Fanshawe. Loggy Hole Farm continued being prosperous. In addition to food crops, it became well known for prize cattle, assorted livestock, and thoroughbred horses.

Why would any landowner burden his property with such an unattractive name? It must be considered that the name was derived from a unique feature of the property. Perhaps as early as the 1800's there were numerous downed trees across a portion of the land. It is likely that tides might have strewn debris along the marshy river banks, and storms likely swashed the rubble onto the farmland itself.

Others theorize that since the area was originally Dutch colony, the term loggy, originated from the Dutch term, log, which means heavy or slow in movement. It is plausible that the farm got its name from the section of land adjacent to the Shrewsbury wetlands where marshes, bogs, and quicksand can be found. Here the marshy land is so weighted with water that it could readily be called " loggy". Since we do not know who named the farm, or his rational for doing so, it remains just another part of the mystery that surrounds Loggy Hole Farm.

We do know, however, that documents of the 1860's mention the existence of quicksand on the property. Quicksand, or as the Bible calls it "sinking sand" is found all around the world, especially near water formations and coastal regions. Early colonists were often warned of quicksand sites by the Lenape. Those who did not heed the warning often discovered it them themselves, sometimes with tragic consequences. Earliest records identify many of these quagmires in the region. By the time of the Civil War, many quicksand pockets were mapped.

As communities grew along the Navesink and Shrewsbury Rivers quicksand became an infrastructure issue. As far back as 1890 the Daily Register reported that Red Bank was dealing with quicksand issues when several newly laid water pipes disappeared into a quicksand cavity. In 1919, Red Bank was forced to deal with quicksand damage once again to underground sewer and water pipes.

Likewise, in Rumson a lengthy section of sewers being laid along Rumson Roads in 1883 vanished into the quicksand soon after it was installed. Shortly afterwards a fox hunter rode his horse into a quagmire during a fox hunt with deadly results. Over the years local authorities discovered that if underground construction is not carefully planned, quicksand will undo their efforts.

Other communities such as Middletown, Shrewsbury, Little Silver, and Oceanport have not been immune to similar infrastructure issues. Today engineers take great care to ensure that all underground utility and public works projects avoid areas of potential quicksand deposits.

Unlike people of the 18th and 19th century who needed to be constantly aware of its dangers, those of us living on the heavily populated peninsula today have little concern about quicksand. We usually associate quicksand with B movies, where the villain gets his just desserts while attempting to escape authorities. But quicksand has been a local concern for many years.

The conundrum of Loggy Hole Farm does not lie with the quicksand issue alone. But when combined with a series of baffling paranormal events on the property, one is left with a most peculiar puzzle.

During the mid-1800's Loggy Hole Farm was a bustling and successful homestead. With its sizable labor force, it produced an assortment of fruits and vegetables as well as breeding both cattle and horses. In addition, it was a common practice for a farm to keep a kennel of hunting hounds. Loggy Hole Farm was no exception. Their hunting hounds were known to be one of the best trained hunting packs in the area

One gray morning Milton Giest, the farmhand who had the sole responsibility for the dogs, finished feeding the hounds and opened the gate to the outside fenced kennel which adjoined their enclosed shelter. The dogs bounded into the fresh air and began running about playfully nipping at one another. Milton was cleaning the inside shelter when he first heard a low whimpering sound coming from the dogs. This quickly grew into barks, growls, snarls, and finally the distinctive bay of the hunting dogs.

Milton turned toward the sound of the ruckus just in time to see the pack leader, General, throw his body against the outside gate. The spring catch snapped and General bounded out of the kennel with the entire pack of hounds on his heels. The dogs bolted away with General in the lead, racing toward the outer pasture toward the river.

Milton shouted, but to no avail. He jumped on a barrel to see where they were headed just in time to see the pack chasing a smoky gray animal along the outer fence line. He squinted to get a better look at the creature the dogs were chasing. He saw a silvery gray body with a long snout just inches ahead of the pack. He looked again, it was certainly not the common a red fox known to inhabit the area. It was grayish, almost white. But Milton knew it couldn't be wolf as it lacked the profile and distinctive wolf like head.

The creature darted through the outer fence followed by the pack of hounds nipping at his tail. Milton gasped and began running as fast as his legs could carry him. The dogs were headed towards the river, towards the quicksand mire on the far edge of the farm.

By the time, he reached the quagmire the silvery invader had disappeared. Instead he found several dogs thrashing about at the edge of the quicksand. He could pull a few hounds to safety. But the dog in the center of the mire, the owner's prize dog, General, thrashed about frantically unable to free himself, until he was gone.

When Milton reported the incident to the foreman a search was made to find and kill the intruder. When it was not found, Milton was accused of drinking on the job. The foreman was furious." Everyone knows that the fox in this area are red, not gray or white."

"I know that," Milton said. "But that is what it looked like."

"The foreman glared at Milton. "You know perfectly well that these hounds would have run away from a wolf, not towards it. Not without encouragement."

Milton was promptly fired.

Although life was soon back to normal on Loggy Hole Farm, rumors began to circulate. There were claims of strange lights near the river's edge, and glowing orbs floating near the quagmire. A few farm hands claim to have seen ashen colored animals along the exterior fence line, and once a pet goat simply disappeared.

The 1890's were a prosperous time in Monmouth County. Loggy Hole Farm was no exception. That day in early April of 1894 was overcast, but the air was warm and everyone sensed that spring had come at last. Loggy Hole Farm had increased its herd of horses and had begun breeding quality animals for sale. One of the prized horses was a chestnut mare named Bernadette.

She was a beautiful horse with a friendly disposition and fine muscular features. The last time she was seen alive she had been out on the outer pasture happily munching on the new sprouts of sweet grass. Although the mare was quiet and calm, a larger gray horse pranced and circled around the mare, frequently lifting his nose and snorting. Then the larger horse began to nip at the mare and she began darting about in a circle trying to escape. No matter which direction she ran, the gray horse cut her off and she had to retreat.

William, the caretaker's son, stood watching the horses for a few minutes. Although he was only nine, he had been around farm animals his whole life and he knew something wasn't right. He hurried into the barn where his father was putting down fresh hay for the animals.

"Pa," he said, "That big gray horse is chasing Bernadette all around the field."

"What are you talking about boy? Bernadette is always in the pasture alone now, you know she is about to foal." But William insisted that a large grey horse was chasing the pregnant mare. Pa dropped his hay rake and ran toward the pasture. When he reached the gate, it stood wide open, the pasture was empty, Bernadette was gone.

The caretaker scoured the nearby field for the mare. In the distance, he thought he saw her disappear through the outer fence into the wetlands with a large gray horse nipping at her hind quarters. He shouted for help and instantly half a dozen farm hands joined the chase. When they reached the outer enclosure, they could see where the horses had crashed through the fencing. They were headed toward the river, toward the swampy area near the quicksand cavity.

When they reached the morass, the gray horse had disappeared. The mare however, thrashed and struggled as the mud enveloped her within moments. She was unable to utter a sound. Despite both an intense search of the property, the gray horse was never seen again.

Word quickly spread of the phantom beasts that seemed to be luring helpless animals to their deaths. Attempts were made to fill the quicksand with logs, and rocks, but to no avail. A strong railing was placed around the area, and workers were cautioned to stay out of the area.

For almost ten years there was little new evidence recorded of mysterious happenings, other than an occasional claim of seeing what looked like birds with silvery gray wings flying in the darkness, and reports of strange lights glowing over the mire. There were occasional lost pets, and once a report of a missing drunken farm hand. There was a brief investigation, but it was soon agreed that he had simply left his nagging wife for a local barmaid.

In 1920 however, an event at the farm would make front page of the Register. It was nearly harvest time and the farm busy. There was so much work to be done to complete the harvest and prepare the farm for winter. A full contingent of hands were at work that morning.

About eleven o clock the lady of the house returned from a visit to a sick neighbor. The driver, Clyde, dropped her off at the front door of the farm house and the drove the two-wheeled buggy to the stable. He hopped from the driver's seat and gently dropped the reins, 'You stay here Beauty" he said." I'll have you unhitched in a minute." He moved to the stable door and stepped inside.

At that moment, there was a loud snort and terrified whinny. Clyde pushed open the door just in time to see the horse bucking and flaying his forelegs at a crouched black creature. Out of the corner of his eye Clyde caught the unmistakable sight of a huge black dog. Later he would recall that it appeared to be bigger than any dog he had ever seen, and he was certain it was not a wolf.

The great beast snarled at the horse showing it long ragged teeth. Still hitched to the buggy the terrified horse bolted across the field and crashed through the fence on the far side. The buggy bounced and wobbled as the horse drug it into the swamp. Close behind was the unmistakable form of a huge black dog.

"Come on!" Clyde shouted to the workers. "Get the gun, it's gonna kill the horse.

When the farm hands reached the mire, there was no sight of the dog. The horse was up to its hocks in mud, and the buggy was overturned in the quicksand pulling the horse towards the depths. The men began slashing the reins to unhitching the terrified horse. They were able to lead it to safety, but not before the carriage sunk to the depth of the morass.

Shotguns in hand the farm crew searched the entire property as well as the neighboring woods. The dog has simply vanished. As word of the event circulated people began gossiping about Loggy Hole Farm. Some claim that it must surely be haunted, others were certain that a demon or witch lived in the swamp.

By 1926 machinery had come to Loggy Hole Farm. A shiny new Farmall tractor was the pride of the farm. The farm hand with sole responsibility for the new machine could not have been happier. Fred considered himself the luckiest man alive when the foreman gave him the job. He kept it in perfect working order and lovingly washed her down every evening, he even had a pet name for her, Fanny, although he never told the other workers.

One spring day he was moving the tractor across the farm from one field to another when he saw a young girl with long flowing hair and a blue bonnet running in a nearby field. It was unusual to see children out in the crop fields. He knew everyone in the family, most of their visitors, and certainly all the crew and their families. But he didn't recognize the little girl.

He slowed the Farmall to an idle and watched the child running near the outer fence near the river. That isn't good he thought, that little one shouldn't be so near the swamp. He shouted a warning to her, but it was drowned out by the noise of the tractor motor.

She stood by the gate for a moment and seemed to stare at Fred. Then she reached up, unattached the gate and disappeared into the scrub grass on the edge of the swamp. He knew he couldn't catch her if he ran, so he put the tractor into high gear and bounced across the pasture as fast as he could. The wind lashed his face as he tried to reach the girl before she entered the wetlands. He thought he saw her blue bonnet just ahead, but then the girl suddenly disappeared. He drove the tractor a bit further through the low shrubs. Looking around he shouted out to the little girl. There was no answer.

At that moment, he felt the two small front tires of the tractor slide into muddy slime. Fred gasped, he had driven into the quicksand. The Farmall began to slide, within moments the motor died. Fred leapt from the sinking tractor, landing just along the edge of the quicksand. He hit hard, his right knee spouting blood. He looked across the quagmire and watched as the beautiful new tractor began to sink into the sludge. Soon just the tip of giant back tires was still in sight. He scanned the area for the child, but she was gone.

When he reported the incident, his boss insisted he had been drinking, and insisted that there were no little girls playing in the fields. The next day Fred went looking for a new job.

We may think that the series of paranormal events which occurred at Loggy Hole Farm were rare manifestations. However, the opposite is true. Claims of peculiar forms, strange entities, lights, and mysterious animals which guide others from a safe path to place of doom have been reported throughout history and across the globe.

In many English speaking cultures the phenomena is sometimes called will-0'-wisp, which takes its name from Medieval Latin for "foolish fire." Across the globe, especially in areas of bogs, swamps, and marshes flickering lights or grayish animal or human forms are reported. They are always associated with a variety of peculiar events where the innocent are steered to tragedy by some mysterious form.

In America, they are commonly called ghost lights, or death orbs. Nearly every culture on the globe has such phenomena with its own distinctive name and similar description. Although each culture has unique characteristics, in each case, the malevolent spirt leads the innocent to its doom. In Asia, it is a phenomenon named Aleya. In Japan, a similar creature known as Chir batti is seen. The Min Min of Australia, the Pixie of Cornwall, the Spunkie of Scotland, the Brujas of Mexico, and the Weisse Frauen Kin of Germany are a few of the names given these enigmatic elemental spirits.

Although we must admit that the events at Loggy Hole Farm are not unique, they do remain perplexing, a puzzle, indeed a conundrum. Just as with other world cultures we are left to identify the culprit. Is it some form of haunting, a shape changer, a demonic presence, or a curse on the land? Or is it something else?

Who is to say what may be going on within the housing developments that grace what was once Loggy Hole Farm? Where are the missing pets? Why do residents call authorities complaining of peculiar lights in the sky and grayish shadows along the water front? Is it swamp gas, or some other natural phenomena? Or do the spirits that plagued Loggy Hole Farm linger still?

An Apparition In The Ice

nother anecdote from the long and colorful history of the Navesink River unites a period of great excitement on the Navesink with a local tragedy resulting in an unexplained series of events.

About the time of the Civil War, as the nation struggled to stay united, a new and exciting winter sport was born right here on the Navesink. Although the ice sled had been used to transport supplies for some time by both Europeans and the early American colonists; its use as a recreational vehicle first gained popularity here on the Navesink.

George Allaire and Nathan Cook are credited with building and sailing their first Navesink iceboat in 1865. It immediately became the talk of the entire waterfront. It wasn't long before others joined in the frosty adventure. Soon a multitude of homemade boats of every conceivable style and form were sharing the frozen river. Everyone seemed to have their own favorites, but eventually the three runner masted boat became the most popular model. Almost immediately iceboats were being commercially produced.

It wasn't long before the Navesink gained national attention. People came from great distances to both participate and observe the iceboaters on the frozen river. By 1880 an iceboat club, the North Shrewsbury Ice Boat and Yacht Club, was formed. Soon, weather permitting, the river was alive with the sound of flapping sails and the scratch of runners gliding atop the icy river. There were races between the two bridges, winter ice carnivals, and regattas. Even Thomas A. Edison brought his newly invented movie camera to Red Bank three times between 1900-1903 to film the iceboats in action.

Iceboating remains extremely popular, hampered only by a recent trend to warmer winters. The significance of iceboating cannot be overstated. The official emblem of Red Bank features a large iceboat under sail. The North Shrewsbury Iceboat and Yacht Club is still going strong.

Organizers from the club have been instrumental in developing and maintaining safety on the river. During the iceboating season, there are hourly depth checks, temperature monitoring, clearly identified course paths, as well as hazard warning signs and even boat inspections. Every possible effort is made to insure safety on the ice.

There were of course numerous minor mishaps and crashes over the years, but nothing serious ensued until February 12, 1906. That Sunday morning was bitterly cold. The ice had been frozen solid for several days. When the wind picked up that morning iceboating enthusiasts headed for the river.

The Navesink appeared to be solid off the Fair Haven dock when Charles and Benjamin Hendrickson hurried to join the dozens of other iceboaters taking advantage of the smooth glistening ice. Bundled in long johns, two layers of clothes as well as heavy coats, gloves, scarves and heavy wool hats, the two brothers set out for a fun day on the river.

With the younger brother, Benjamin as pilot, they sped up and down the river with the icy wind smacking their faces. They were both laughing so hard they failed to keep a sharp look out for thin ice. Without warning their boat crashed through a soft spot in the ice plunging the two brothers head first into the icy water.

Benjamin escaped by clinging to the windward runner, but his brother was not so lucky. Charles was plunged deep into the icy Navesink. Despite his brother's valiant efforts to save him, he was trapped beneath the ice and drowned.

It was an emotional scene as rescuers used oyster tongs to drag the area of the river where the boy fell in. After about an hour his lifeless body was returned to the surface. Despite attempts of resuscitation, Charles was pronounced dead at the scene.

For some years after the event numerous witnesses allege to have seen an apparition of the drown teen frozen in the ice. The grotesque apparition is seen only in early February when the temperatures are the most frigid. Witnesses maintain that the face of the drowned victim is smeared against the ice contorted in pain and fear. Some claim to hear garbled cries for help from beneath the ice. Others insist that they were so terrified they fled the river, leaving their iceboats behind.

By 1940 there were many versions to the story, few of which reflected the true details from the newspaper accounts of the event. Although fathers and grandfathers retold the story repeatedly to warn their sons of the dangers of thin ice, it never dampened the youngsters' enthusiasm for iceboating.

Frank and Burt were no exception. The eleven-year-old twins had lived their entire lives along the Navesink. They swam there before they could walk, sailed homemade rafts they had built from scraps of lumber, and during the summer dug clams with their father for their evening supper. The boys loved fishing, swimming, sailing, and especially iceboating. They loved to do anything that had to do with the river, and any activity that did not involve long division or Reverend Formans's long sermons.

Frank and Burt had heard all the different accounts of the accident but didn't believe a single word of the claims by those who claimed to see the apparition. Just the week before they had scoffed at a classmate, Billy, who claimed his uncle had seen the apparition of the drowned boy.

It had been a mild winter, so when the deep chill first appeared in early February the boys became eager for the first iceboating of the winter. They hurried to the iceboat shed every afternoon right after school and began preparing the ice boat for its first run of the winter. There was wood to polish and blades to sharpen. The twins were finishing their work on the blades when Frankie tossed his rag into the air, "I've got it!" he exclaimed. Although Burt was the older twin, by at least ten full minutes, it was Frankie, the younger who first can up with the idea.

"You got what?" Burt looked up at his brother and frowned. He knew that look on Frankie's face. That look usually meant trouble.

"I know how to get even with Billy." Frankie crowed, "I'll fix him. He even had the girls crowding around him when he bragged about his uncle seeing the face in the ice." Burt's face took on a worried look, before he could speak Frankie went on, "We'll tell everyone that we saw the face ourselves. That's better than some dumb uncle seeing it."

"I d, d, d, don't know Frankie," Burt countered.

"Stop stuttering," Frank commanded. "It's a great idea. Listen, you don't have to talk at all, all you do is stand there. Nod your head while I am talking and agree to everything I say. Got it?"

The frown on Burt's face softened, "Are you sure it will work? We could get into a lot of trouble."

"Of course, it will work, I got it all figured out. I'll lay it on thick too, we'll scare the girls good." Frankie gleefully grabbed his polishing cloth and continued polishing the iceboat.

The next morning Frankie was already in homeroom when the bell rang. As his classmates filed in, the room filled with chatter, laughter, and the sound of bodies plopping into chairs. "Hey Billy, that face your uncle saw on the ice is a fake," Frankie shouted above the din. "Burt and I saw the real one. It was nothing like that sorry one you claim your uncle saw." Burt swallowed hard and took a deep breath, Frankie was at it again.

"Oh yeah? I don't believe it? So, what did it look like?" Billy taunted.

Although Frankie was speaking to Billy, thirty sets of eyes locked onto Frankie. As he began to speak the class eased from their chairs and moved closer and closer until they formed a circle around Frankie and Billy. Frankie began to speak hurriedly. "Well, two nights ago, it was nearly dark. Burt and I went to check to see if the ice was ready for the weekend."

"Your Dad didn't let you do that," Billy challenged. "Only grownups do ice checks."

"Do you want to hear about the monster or not?" Frankie asked.

Murmurs of, "Monster! what monster?" bounced around the room.

"We were out on the ice looking for soft spots, over by the old pilings on the north side and that is when we heard the moan." Frankie said

"You said, you saw it," Billy interrupted.

"We did, but we heard it first. It moaned like someone was stabbing it with a sword, and then it screamed bloody murder! It was coming from under the ice. I kid you not. Right Burt?" Burt managed a small nod of his head.

"It was horrible, like something suffering and angry at the same time. But then we looked at the ice and saw it. The group gasped and two of the girls hugged one another."

"Go on!" someone urged.

"There it was, a face, well kind of a face." Frankie paused to let it sink it. "It kind of looked human, but it wasn't really human. It was like a dead goat or maybe, or a bear with hatchet marks all over it, and no, more like a dead body all rotten and jelly like." Moans filled the air.

"The face of whatever it is was smeared up against the ice and it was looking right at us. There were purple scars with maggots and blood oozing from its squashed nose. The eyes were out of their sockets and bulged as if coming right out of the ice. There was green glowing slime everywhere and the eye balls followed us when we moved."

Frankie knew he had their undivided attention now. He began describing how a moaning screechy voice came from the grotesque creature, pleading, "Children, children, I want children, bring me children." The boys looked at one another with wide eyes, several girls screamed and Molly and Patty ran crying from the room.

"It was the most grotesque and disgusting thing you ever saw. And smell, did I tell you it smelled like an old outhouse." Frankie added. "And you know what was the worst part was that...."

At that moment, Miss Price entered the class room with Molly and Patty in tow. Her normal smile was upside down, "Franklin, what is going on?"

Frankie froze, he could feel her eyes fixed on him. "What did you do to make these girl cry?" she demanded.

Frankie gave her his most innocent look. "Oh, it was nothing, Miss Price. I was just telling everyone that Burt and me saw the apparition on the river."

"That is Burt and I, young man, watch your grammar." She turned to the class, "Everyone to your seats. Now! "Instantly the circle melted as everyone hurried to their seats. Burt crept into his chair trying to make himself invisible.

"Frankie, I don't want to hear another word about that superstition. Do you understand?"

"Yes, Miss Price. I was only…."

"Not another word! "Miss Price turned to face Burt, who was huddled so tightly in his seat that he had nearly turned himself into a ball," Were you in on this as well, Burt?"

Burt tried to answer, but he could only stutter, "I, I, I, I"

"Never mind, Burt," her voice softened.

"Boys, I will be speaking with you father about this. And when I do I will mention those dreadful spelling tests last week." It was the longest afternoon either boy could ever remember. But the night would be even longer.

When Frankie and Burt arrived home after school their father was waiting for them at the front door. "Hey Dad, you're home early," Frankie exclaimed.

"Don't you hey Dad me, mister! Both of you get in this house this instant!" The boys looked at one another, anytime their parents used their full names they knew there was trouble. They slowly followed their father to the living room.

As expected their father scolded them both for disrupting class, for making the girls cry, and especially for making up stories. Not only was he deeply disappointed in the two sons that bore his name, but the entire family was embarrassed by their actions. He seemed to go on and on even longer than Reverend Forman's sermons.

Finally, their father told them the consequence for their disgraceful conduct in school. The planned iceboating day on the river this Sunday was cancelled. When Frankie started to protest, his father warned, "I am not done yet, young man." In addition, the boys would be dropped off at church on Sunday morning. They would attend both the long worship service, Sunday school, and then would help Mrs. Murphy with the refreshments for the coffee hours, and clean up the church hall afterwards. They would be there at least four hours.

"We were just…" Frankie tried to speak.

"Stop, no excuses," their father said. "Since I can't ice boat alone I will take your Mother for a nice Sunday brunch down along the shore.

We will be back in the afternoon. When you finish helping Mrs. Murphy cleaning up the church hall, you will walk her home, and take her dog for its afternoon walk, and do any chores she may have for you."

"Dad! That reverend talks for hours and hours, and Mrs. Murphy, that dog of her's stinks."

"Enough!" Dad shouted and walked away.

The twins looked at one another, could there have been any worse punishment?

The next day was Saturday morning, and that meant it was chore day for everyone. The boys were grim as they started their tasks, now they had nothing to look forward to the entire weekend. Their father had barely spoken to them at all except to remind them they needed to have all their chores done by supper time.

As the boys were gathering logs for the fireplace Frankie muttered to himself about the unfairness of the punishment. He grabbed a fireplace log and tossed it to Burt, who caught it and stacked in the log shuttle.

"It isn't fair! This is the first good ice of the winter and we are going to miss it, all just because some dumb girl was blubbering all over the teacher."

"I don't know, Burt sighed, "You did make it sound scary. There must be some way we could convince Dad to take us iceboating tomorrow, maybe if we promised never ever again to make the girls cry."

"Nah," Frankie said," that won't work."

Frankie was quiet for a few minutes and then he shrieked, "I got it! I know how we can go iceboating!"

"Frankie, no way, we can't go iceboating, Dad said so,".

"Here's the plan Burt, just listen." As they worked Frankie laid out his plan. First, when they went back inside Frankie would sneak up stairs while Burt was loading the log shuttle. He would gather all their iceboating clothes, jackets, pants, boots, gloves and hats and tie them into one of their bed sheets. Burt's eyes were wide and he kept shaking his head back and forth.

Frankie ignored him and explained that they would work hard and finish all the chores. After supper, they would volunteer to do the dishes and clean up the kitchen for Mom. Then while they were doing that Frankie will sneak up and toss the ball of out the window onto lawn. "Then when we take out the garbage, we'll grab the clothes and stash them in the iceboat until tomorrow." Burt let out a soft moan.

"The rest will be easy," Frankie continued. "We'll dress up and go to church, just like Dad said. As soon as Dad leaves we 'll double back home, and go iceboating. Mom and Dad won't be home till late afternoon."

"Oh, I don't know Frankie, it sounds complicated," Burt mumbled.

"It's perfect. We'll have time for a couple great rides on the ice, and still have time to come back and change back into our Sunday clothes," Frankie smiled at his plan. "Never mind, all you need to do is back me up, no matter what happens."

Everything went according to plan. When Frankie and Burt offered to do the clean-up for mom, she gave them such a smile. "My sweet boys, I'm so proud of you," she cooed, giving each a kiss on the forehead before hurrying to join their father in the living room.

Quick as they could they did all the dishes and cleaned the kitchen. While Burt scrubbed the last of the pots, Frankie crept upstairs and tossed the bag of iceboat clothes out the bedroom window onto the lawn. With that done they hurried to take out the garbage. They snatched the bag of clothes from the lawn and quickly stashed the bundle in the iceboat.

It was even colder the next morning when Burt and Frankie were dropped off in front of the church just before nine o o'clock. They were dressed in their Sunday best. Mom kept saying how handsome they looked, and Dad gave them money for the collection. He reminded them they must stay for both services and to help Mrs. Murphy with refreshments for coffee hour. Finally, he added, "And one more thing boys, no snowball fights in your good clothes, and only one piece of cake, even if they offer you more. Got it?"

"Yes, sir," they answered in unison.

The boys waved goodbye to their parents and walked slowly up the steps of the church. They stepped aside to let an older couple enter. Just as the door closed Frankie grabbed Burt by the sleeve and yanked him along as he darted into the evergreen shrubbery which surrounded the building. They sat among the thick greens until they were sure no one had seen them. They moved quickly through the prickly underbrush until they reached the corner near the rear parking lot. They darted across the lawn and onto the street. From there they doubled back, being careful to avoid neighbors.

When they got to their house they ran straight to the iceboat shed. The temperature was in the twenties and the boys shivered as they changed into their winter clothes. "Frankie, you didn't bring our long johns, we're gonna freeze." Burt grumbled.

Frankie was dressed by then and opened the doors to the ice shed as Burt finished getting his boots tied. He rushed to the water's edge and then ran out onto ice sliding until he fell over. He smacked the ice hard with his fist, "See!" he yelled to Burt, "Solid as a rock. Come on, we'll just do a couple rides, put the boat back, and be back home before Mom and Dad."

"Are you sure we should do this alone?" Burt asked

"You're a such an old Nelly. What are you talking about? Look at the river, there are a dozen boats out there already, come on time is a wasting."

They shoved and tugged and finally with one big yank slid the iceboat out on to the frozen Navesink. Frankie pushed the boat farther out on to the river for a better position while Burt carefully adjusted the sail so it would catch the wind, just as his father had taught him,

The boat began to glide across the ice. Frankie jumped into the pilot seat. "Come on, Burt, get onboard." he called. Burt caught hold of the mast and swung himself into position. The instant he adjusted the sail the little boat seemed to take flight. The boys were hurtling down the river faster than they had ever done before.

Suddenly loud curses came at them from another boat. "Watch where you are going! You're going to kill somebody!" The boys had been laughing so hard they had paid little attention to the other iceboats on the river.

"You got to steer!" Burt shouted.

"I'm trying, I'm trying!" Frankie screeched. Just then he looked ahead and saw a much larger boat bearing down on them. It was directly ahead and coming in fast. Frankie yanked on the tiller as hard as he could and the little boat went sideways, toward the far bank. At that moment a cross wind swept the boat around in a circle and the boys flew from the boat and landed on the hard ice.

Frankie sat up first and searched for his brother. Burt lay on the ice near the overturned boat. Frankie held his breath as he approached, just then Burt sat up, rubbing a scrape on his chin. Frankie whooped, "That was some ride, wasn't it?"

"Let's hope we didn't wreck the boat," Burt muttered as he began to inspect the mast. After deciding they needed to get the craft upright Frankie moved around to the other side of the boat to help lift.

"OK," Frank ordered," When I say three you lift your side"

Frankie had just counted to two when Burt saw it. "Fr..fra., fran, frank k, k, eee..frakkkie!" Burt shrieked and dropped the boat onto the ice.

"Come on you donkey, I can't lift this by myself, I..." Frankie never finished.

"You better come, come over here…" Bert screeched.

Frankie muttered to himself as he let the boat gently back onto the ice. He looked at his brother who was shaking like a leaf and pointing to a spot on the ice. "Don't tell me we broke it," Frankie said as he hurried to where Bert was standing.

Then, he saw it too. There it was, the face. Not just any face, that face. It was the very same face Frankie had described in school. Then from the ice, just a few feet from the boat came a moaning sound, it sounded like someone being stabbed by a sword, and then it screamed. It screamed and screamed, it screamed bloody murder!

The boys were frozen in place. The creature looked like it was suffering terribly, and at the same time was angry and vengeful. The face, if you can call it a face, was kind of human, but not human. It was kind of like a goat, sort of a bear whose face was sliced by a hatchet. It had the expression of a dead body, all rotten and jelly like.

The face of whatever it is was smeared into the ice and was glaring right at the boys. There were purple scars with maggots and blood oozing from its squashed nose. The eyes were out of the sockets and bulged as if they were coming right out of the ice. There was a green glowing slime everywhere and the eye balls stared at the boys. A pungent smell seemed to be seeping up from the ice, a smell not unlike an old outhouse.

Just then a loud moaning voice beckoned from the grotesque face, "Children, children, come here children."

The two could not take their eyes off the monstrous form. The more they stared the brighter the face became, and then it started to move. At the same moment, an unearthly bellow erupted from the beneath the ice, "Children, children, now I have children!"

"Let's get out of here, "Frankie shrieked as he bolted toward the shore with Burt close behind. The boys ran and never looked back. They fell a few times on the ice but jumped up and kept on running. They ran the whole way home, and didn't even to stop at the iceboat shed for their Sunday clothes.

A longtime later:

After facing the local police and their very angry parents,

After hauling the heavy iceboat across the river by themselves while being lectured by their irate father,

After watching as a shiny new padlock was placed on the door of the iceboat house,

After hearing a sermon from their dad that was twice as long as Reverend Forman's had ever been,

After they ate supper at a silent dinner table and were sent to their room while the family had dessert.

After all that, Frankie and Burt sat quietly staring out their bedroom window at the Navesink.

"Dad says the boat is damaged and we won't be doing any iceboating this winter," Burt sighed.

"Yeah, and they had coconut custard pie for dessert, that is my all-time favorite," Frankie answered.

"Yeah, I know," Burt said. "But we did see it.

"I know, but no one believes us." Frankie walked to window and opened it allowing a gush of cold air into the room. The icy breeze brought a peculiar stench.

"That stinks, close the window," Burt ordered.

Frankie looked out onto the frozen Navesink. Just as he did a single lonely iceboat glided down river, its white sail reflected by the full moon. The face of the pilot was unusually large and seemed to cast a green glow. It was then Frankie was certain he heard someone laugh and call out "Children, children, I want children."

Ghostly Spirits of the
Twin Gables Speakeasy

When we think of the Prohibition era in our history one of the first words which comes to mind is the speakeasy. It doesn't matter what they were called: gin mill, saloon, blind pig, tea room, birds' nest, restaurant, hotel, or simply a club. Between 1920 and 1933, anywhere illegal alcohol was served became known as a speakeasy.

The origin of the term seems obvious, a speakeasy would describe a location where you are required to speak softly, therefore in an "easy," manner, as not to be discovered. Although this is indeed the general meaning of the term, there are numerous claims to its origin.

In the nineteenth century, the term was used for any meeting place where an illegal activity might be going on. This included both drinking as well as smuggling. It was used frequently by well-known Irish smugglers. Other claims insist it was first used in Pennsylvania, where even today townships and cities can declare themselves "dry." (Alcohol is not sold within the boundaries of the community.) The term was first seen here in print in the 1840's, when speakeasies began popping up across the Commonwealth.

In the early days of Prohibition speakeasies were known as blind pigs. This claim originates in Maine, where a man with an illegal speakeasy kept a blind pig in his back room. He sold tickets for a quarter to see the blind pig in his back room. In addition to viewing the blind animal, the patron received a glass of rum. The term, blind pig, soon became a popular synonym for a speakeasy.

Across the nation people came up with a wide variety of names as well as creative schemes to camouflage their sale of illegal brew. Regardless of what you called it, the illegal drinking establishments didn't just ignite during Prohibition, they literally exploded across the nation. There was hardly a town or city without some sort of a speakeasy. By 1930 the term was part of the American lexicon.

A speakeasy could be anything from a fancy nightclub club to an individual's home selling booze in a backroom or basement. It could be a secret bar in a business such as a restaurant, hotel, grocery store, garage, hardware, or even a funeral home. They were found in cellars, hidden rooms, and roof tops. At one time, there were 100,000 in New York City, and our Jersey shore was dotted with such watering holes.

Lower class speakeasies could be as simple as an elderly lady selling "tea" each afternoon to local ladies; to some truly rough and tumble spots where the danger of being caught by the IRS was the least of a patron's concerns. They could be simple, or have complicated disguises with anything from the infamous blind pig, to a dance hall or a musical presentation. Here, the booze might be called coffin varnish, white mules, monkey rum, squirrel juice, rot gut, tangle foot or just hooch. The liquor was almost always diluted, sometimes with water and more often with an industrial chemical intended to mask the dilution.

They were none the less, highly secretive. They nearly always required the hopeful drinker to identify a hidden pass word or other secret signal to be admitted. Some, such O'Leary's in the Bowery of New York, was claimed to be "not for the squeamish". Others focused on sporting events, ethnic societies, or even political or civic associations.

The genteel classes who frequented high-end speakeasies rarely referred to them as such. They were known as clubs or parties. This form of speakeasy began to flourish as organized crime became involved in the business. Early on, the upper crust began holding elaborate house parties where they could serve illegal alcohol in privacy. This was less profitable to the bootlegger as fewer individuals bought booze, and less frequently.

Speakeasies, many supported by organized crime, known as clubs multiplied across the nation. They provided a place for people to entertain friends, listen to live music, see a stage show, and have elegantly prepared meals. The clubs went to great lengths to entice women to attend, bringing the first "powder rooms" to public drinking establishments. From these clubs the term night club arose.

The famous Cotton Club in Harlem, as well as the Bath Club, and New York's 21 Club have been the subject of numerous books and movies. The Cotton Club brought jazz to the general population, while the Bath Club provided classical concerts each evening. Here at the shore, several of the remaining posh beach hotels provided guests and locals with similar accommodations. High end clubs employed elaborate security methods to protect themselves from raids.

Raids of speakeasies by the federal revenues was always an issue. Wide spread corruption among politicians and the police was so rampant that the speakeasy often had advance notice of the upcoming raid. The famous 21 Club had a complicated security system in which the man at the door could push a button and the entire bar would disappear, while the booze emptied into the sewer.

In both the upper and lower class speakeasies the quality of the liquor was always questionable. Before Prohibition one could order a specific brand and expect to be served that brand. During Prohibition, you might order by brand, but you got whatever the bootlegger was serving, even if he called it by your brand's name. It was inevitably a lower quality liquor, and most likely diluted. Only the well-connected received the actual real product. Even Joseph P. Kennedy, well known businessman and head of the famous political Kennedy clan, had to resort to serving "treated gin' to his former Harvard classmates guests in 1924. He reportedly noted that they were happily fooled by his substitution.

Another trick of the trade was to sell, at premium prices, what they called "overboard stuff." This was low quality gin, poured into Gordon gin bottles, and then disguised to look as if he had been tossed overboard during a rum runners' escape, and later recovered. This particular trick was reported to have been practiced right here in Red Bank in a local bottling plant.

Companies in Europe created "brands" such as Cutty Sark and Haig and Haig just for the bootleg American market. It was during this era that many cocktails still popular today were "invented." This was done to disguise the taste of chemically treated booze. Pink ladies, brandy alexanders, gin rickeys, sidecars, bee's knees, and Mary Pickford's, are just a few cocktails developed to hide the disagreeable taste of the chemically treated booze. In addition, the colorful names served to entice the ladies to the clubs.

Americans continued their love affair with alcohol despite Prohibition. Not only did it not slow down the sale of liquor, it also eliminated a major source of revenue for the government, as taxes and tariffs on alcohol could no longer be collected.

Here along the shore speakeasies dotted the landscape. They could be found in Long Branch, Sea Bright, Monmouth Beach, Little Silver, Red Bank, Middletown, and Rumson. Some targeted the working class and were found in back rooms, basements, businesses, rooming houses, and small hotels. Others were high-end clubs or "parties" held in big homes along the beach, as well as in elegant "restaurants" and "hotels" all along our shores.

The cast of characters of speakeasy owners is as vast as the kind and number of speakeasies. Mom and pop stores, businesses with hidden rooms, little old lady tea shops, hardware stores, fish markets, lumberyards, bakeries, and even funeral homes were once speakeasies. Organized crime took the speakeasy to an entire new level offering services and entertainment equivalent to that of the modern casino.

Speakeasies were as diverse as their patron lists. Some speakeasies catered to specific classes of people, others to those in certain forms of business, others to certain ethnicities, and some to anyone at all. The Prohibition era found interesting new social mixing. Now women drank openly in the company of other men and women. Speakeasies catered to women in many ways, encouraging them with special powder rooms, dainty drinks, and handsome attentive waiters. It was also the era when the races first began to mix socially. Early on these were known as black and tan clubs. Here jazz and ragtime were introduced to the general population.

According to most historians, Americans have always been heavy drinkers. As early as 1791 Alexander Hamilton realized that taxing alcohol would be a solid source of income for the new American government. And indeed, it was. By 1862 the revenue brought in by the sale of liquor was 20% of the federal budget, no small figure. Some say the Union could not have fought the Civil War without the revenue collected from alcohol taxes. It is estimated that between 1920 and 1933 the government lost a minimum of 250 million dollars a year from the loss of tax on liquor.

To many Americans, who were not happy about Prohibition to begin with, it was an opportunity of a life time. Here at the Jersey Shore local rum runners provided a constant supply of imported liquor. The heavily populated cities of the East Coast provided the demand as well as the market. Some saw it as a win-win situation.

Nearly every little town along the Navesink and Shrewsbury Rivers, not to mention the North Shore, had a throng of speakeasies during Prohibition. Today, Murphy's, a popular Rumson tavern, was once one of the area's most successful speakeasies. Located on an isolated cove on the Navesink it was a favorite watering hole for locals during Prohibition. Other speakeasies flourished across the two-river region. In the Italian community of Red Bank, located along Shrewsbury Avenue, speakeasies flourished within the numerous rooming houses, mom and pop stores, businesses, hotels, and restaurants.

Naturally the completion among the secretive speakeasies sometimes fostered theft, intimidation, hijackings, and even murder. In January 1923, the New York Times referred to Highlands as "bootlegger haven", and identified Atlantic Highlands as the center of organized crime's smuggling efforts.

Organized crime families frequently operated openly on the streets of Red Bank's Westside. Vito Genovese, local mob boss, narrowly escaped an assassin's bullets while entering the Abbott Hotel speakeasy on Shrewsbury Avenue in the early 1920's. The New York assassin was not as fortunate, as he was found a week later in a ditch along Seven Bridges Road riddled in bullet holes. The local violence between organized crime families was rampant and the crime families would continue their internal warfare throughout Prohibition.

Red Bank not only housed speakeasies but was also the site of a major bootlegging operation on Pearl Street. The Calandriello brothers used their bottling company to mix single malt with chemicals and water to create "treated gin." In the Fall of 1922 a murder at the site threated the operation for a time.

The speakeasy became a fixture in the community despite their illegality. Many authors claim that many local police departments either looked the other way, or more often were on the payrolls of speakeasies and bootleggers. All too often the speakeasy owner had knowledge of upcoming raids.

Near the end of Prohibition, not only had the speakeasy become part of the American lexicon, but finding a drink became a simple matter. When Prohibition ended in 1933, many speakeasies simply opened their doors publicly and continued in business. Today, many restaurants and bars take advantage of the colorful history of Prohibition and advertise their speakeasy décor.

In the years since the end of Prohibition most the original buildings which housed speakeasies have either been demolished, moved or remodeled. A few remain in private homes, while others took on an entire new lease on life with massive renovations and with totally new businesses. It is not uncommon for building contractors in our area to come across doors or steps to nowhere, hidden rooms, unmarked cellars, and sometimes even an old cache of bottles or brewing paraphernalia.

Those familiar with the paranormal world will attest that it is quite common for ghosts and other supernatural phenomena to be awakened and even antagonized by major remodeling and renovations.

We also know that ghosts are rather territorial and tend to be embedded in one place or a specific building with which they have an emotional connection. There was so much unfinished business, such loss of life, and upheaval during this era, that it is not surprising that the number of hauntings associated with local speakeasies is substantial.

Such was the case shared by an elderly gentleman who once resided at

36 Riverside Avenue, the Twin Gables Apartments. He recalled his experiences at the speakeasy with candor and good humor.

Twin Gables was an imposing four story Tudor apartment building that once graced the banks of the Navesink River here in Red Bank. The stately old building is itself just a ghost now. She has disappeared totally from the landscape of Riverside Avenue, torn down and discarded a few years ago.

I expect she is remembered only by a few long-time locals. In my head, I know she is gone. Yet each time I drive by I don't see that annex from the building next door, I see only the Twin Gables as she once stood, so solidly and proudly overlooking the Navesink.

I can still picture her so clearly. Her dark red brick walls stretched skyward for three floors, interrupted only by a few narrow windows across the front on each floor. At the fourth floor the brick gave way to a white stucco surface which was rimmed with half- timbers in both vertical and diagonal strips. This Tudor design was accented by identical gables on each corner of the building.

Twin Gables not only looked sturdy, but she felt sturdy as well. I always suspected that not even a hurricane could topple the building. Many a nor'easter was barely noticeable from inside the plaster walls of the one and two bedroom apartments. They built the "Gables" back in 1927 when people took building seriously.

That is where we were living when it happened. It all began that winter, that final year that we lived on the river at Twin Gables. I was only a sophomore in high school when my father died. By the time I was a senior my mother had been forced to give up the house in Fair Haven. We took a one bedroom apartment in Twin Gables. Mom really wanted a two-bedroom so we could each have our own room. But it was just too expensive. I was hoping to head off to college that coming Fall, so I planned to sleep on the sofa bed in the living room.

When we looked at the rear apartment on the first floor, I could tell right away that Mom loved it. Sunshine streamed through the bank of windows along the length of the apartment facing the river. Just below the windows a small garden opened into a spectacular view of the Navesink. Although there was a building on each side, they merely served to make the garden more secluded. Despite having just one bedroom, it was a great apartment.

The only drawback was that we needed to be out of the house in a week, and the former residents had left the apartment abruptly and without notice. The rooms were littered with unwanted belongings, old clothes, and trash of all sorts. Along the living room wall the plaster was marred by several large gashes which looked like the wall had exploded from within. The apartment was in shambles.

The super was happy to rent the apartment to us, but he was very busy and said that he couldn't promise that it would be ready for another month. He grumbled about all the trouble he had with the former tenants, the fighting and noise which the other tenants had reported. Now they had left this giant mess.

I could see the disappointment on Mom's face. I offered to haul out all the trash and clean the entire apartment myself. I told him that my uncles would help and that we would do all the repairs and repaint the apartment, if only he would let us take it sooner. His eyes lit up, and he handed me the keys. He even told Mom that she could have the rest of that month rent free because it was one enormous job.

Mom made some phone calls to my uncles and I started cleaning and hauling out trash that very day. Some of my friends came over and helped me haul garbage bag after garbage bag of spoiled food, old boots, clothes, broken rusty appliances, and just plain trash. While we hauled rubbish, Mom scrubbed the kitchen until it shone. By the end of the second day we had the apartment cleaned and ready to spackle and paint.

The only remaining chore was to clean out a closet located in the hall-way which ran between the living room and my mother's bedroom. It was jammed to the ceiling with boxes and books, and all sorts of papers. We decided to ignore it for the time being. We needed to get the apartment painted so we could move it. Cleaning out that last closet shouldn't be any big deal.

I skipped school the next day and met my uncles and two cousins before seven. We patched, plastered, spackled, and sanded. By nightfall we had completely painted the entire apartment. Even the woodwork had a clean new coat of paint. I was so exhausted I could hardly walk, but I felt pleased we had done such a good job.

We moved in the very next day. It didn't take too long, we only had Mom's bedroom furniture, a kitchen table and chairs, and a few pieces of living room furniture. Of course, there were dozens of cardboard boxes. Far too many, we soon realized, to fit into a one bedroom apartment.

Shortly after beginning to unpack we realized we had made a terrible mistake by not cleaning out that hall closet. There was nowhere for my clothes, or any of my things. They had to go into that closet. So, we pushed aside the stack of moving boxes, grabbed more trash bags, and began hauling out the trash from the closet.

It was much deeper than we realized, it was more like a little storeroom. We took out old suitcases, boxes of books, reams of paper tied together with twine, and several large very old photo albums. I was about to toss the albums into a garbage bag when my Mother told me to lay them aside. They were very old and would be very interesting to go through some day.

Mom went to get the vacuum as I reached out to dust off the back wall of the closet. I wasn't sure at first, the closet was deep and there was no light. Something wasn't right. I grabbed a flashlight and went to the rear wall of the closet. To my surprise, it wasn't plaster at all, it was a large wooden door. Why would someone use a door as a wall in a closet? I grabbed hold of the knob and it turned. To my surprise the hinges creaked and ever so slowly the door opened.

I reached out to feel the space and it was empty. It was dark except for a dim shaft of light coming from somewhere along a side wall. Before I could call out Mom returned with the vacuum. We stood there in the dark, not believing our eyes.

We stepped into the dark space without a single spoken word. As I scanned the walls with the flashlight I could see that it was empty, well nearly empty. Through the thick dust, I could make out a counter of some sort along the far wall. The musty odor was overwhelming, and as I swung the flashlight across the room the dust swirled into giant whirlpools.

Mom grabbed me by the arm and jerked me out into the living room. We stared at each other. Wiping the dust from our shoulders we just stood there for a moment unable to speak. A hidden room, the apartment had a hidden room. The super must not have known of it or he would have charged us for the two-bedroom unit.

It wasn't long before we were laughing aloud about our find. We couldn't imagine why anyone would hide the entrance to a second bedroom. Why wouldn't anyone living there use that room? And why didn't the super know about the hidden room? We agreed to clean it up and use it as my bedroom, and above all not to mention it to anyone.

Feeling re-energized, we returned to the dark and dusty space armed with flashlights. I found a light switch near the door and flipped it on. Light, although dimmed by a layer of dust, spewed across the ceiling. Now that we could see the room we were even more astonished than ever.

A narrow counter ran nearly the full length of the far wall. When I looked more closely I saw that it had shelves on the backside. In the bottom corner a crumbling cardboard box held half a dozen small glasses. Behind the counter the walls were roughly patched and had been repainted several times. We inspected the remainder of the room and found only dust, years and years of dust.

Then we turned to the exterior wall, behind the door. Heavy maroon drapes attached at the ceiling covered most of the wall. In the middle was the smallest window I ever saw. It was the tiny kind that people used to put in their bathrooms. The glass had been painted black and huge nails protruded from the wooden frame keeping it firmly closed. What on earth was this room used for? And why had it been blocked off?

We decided we needed to get it cleaned up so we could give it a coat of paint. Then I could rescue my bedroom furniture from my grandfather's garage. The first thing that had to go were those heavy maroon drapes, so full of dust they were practically gray. I gave them a yank, and down came an enormous pile of dusty fabric forming clouds of heavy gray dust. As we turned to look at the wall we gasped in unison.

There behind the door, beneath where the drapes had hung where was a portal of some sort. I had no idea what it was. It was just two small wooden doors protruding from the wall. But Mom knew right away that it was an old dumbwaiter. We pried open the doors and stared into the dark shaft. We couldn't see anything except more dust and empty space. She explained that dumbwaiters were often used in the old days to move heavy items to upper floors. That didn't explain why a hidden room would have a dumbwaiter hidden beneath yards of heavy drapery.

It took some time before we got the mountains of fabric bagged up and put in the garbage. It seemed the more we vacuumed the more dust appeared. Finally, we could run the vacuum one last time. While Mom mopped the floor, I washed the walls as best as I could. We were both exhausted. I crashed on the couch without a second thought of my new bedroom.

In the light of day, the room looked a lot better. It was still rather dark until I replaced the old dusty bulb with a new larger one. Now there was plenty of light, I could see that all the walls were badly marked, dented and had been patched. This room was a real mess.

About then I realized how cold it was in the room. I felt the old iron radiator, it was cold as stone. I bent down and played with the small round knob. It didn't budge at first. Finally, it gave way and I could turn it a full half turn. I sat back and waited. Within a few minutes, I heard a gentle hiss and felt the old radiator begin to heat.

During the next few days we spent our spare time getting the apartment in order. I was getting used to sleeping on the couch. By the weekend, we were ready to start work on the hidden room. We began patching the rough walls and sanding them as smoothly as we could. We used primer on the stains and markings. Finally, we spent all day Sunday giving it a fresh coat of white paint. By midweek I had rescued my bedroom furniture, my catcher's mitt, all my favorite books, and my Star Wars Collection.

I didn't dare toss out the old counter, the super would wonder where it came from. So, I turned it around and used the shelves in the back as a bookcase. I lined up my textbooks and filled most of the other space with my baseball glove, CD collection, and extra sweatshirts. There was still an empty shelf on the bottom so Mom stacked her collection of mystery novels, my baby books, and that dusty old photo album she had rescued from the hall closet. She said that she was going to look through it when she had time.

The apartment could not have been more ideal. It was bright and cheery. Mom seemed to be happy as she decorated and rearranged pictures, pillows, and lamps. There was plenty of room for two people. We overlooked the river from every room except mine. But I didn't mind, I really liked the privacy of my hidden room.

I spent so much time in my room that Mom complained that she never saw me anymore. It was true. I hardly ever used the living room. I could play music in my room and it was barely audible in the rest of the apartment. Best of all was the feeling of privacy. Maybe I should stay home next year and go to community college at Brookdale.

I was having such a great time in my new room that at first I didn't notice it. Yet in the back of my mind I was aware of it for some time before it came to my consciousness. Sometimes I could hear voices, soft mumbling sounds. It was like I was standing outside a church and could hear the people praying aloud. Then I noticed a faint resonance that seemed to be coming from the very center of the room. It wasn't exactly a hum or even a definite melody. It was like music, but a refrain too far away to hear, yet one you recognized.

More than once I stopped what I was doing just to listen for the sound. Sometimes there was nothing but silence. Other times I could distinctly hear a hazy rhythm, or was it music? Then the murmuring started, which was soon followed by a light jangling that I just could not identify. I inspected every room of the apartment. The sounds could not be heard anywhere else in the apartment, only in my room. Of course, I didn't mention it to my mother. I was nearly eighteen, and as the man of the family now I couldn't act like some immature teenager.

It was at the same time I began to feel peculiar. It wasn't exactly a bad feeling, it was a feeling of being, well not quite right. More and more I felt as if I was not alone. It wasn't as if someone was staring at me. It's just that there seemed to be something else present in that room. And sometimes, although the heat was turned on full blast, my room was colder than any other room in the apartment.

To be honest I didn't give it a lot of thought whenever I was away from the apartment. The semester was ending and I was busy doing term papers and projects for school. My social studies elective, History of Monmouth County, had turned out to be more interesting than I expected. Although I had lived along he Navesink my entire life I wasn't aware that so many exciting events had taken place right here in our neighborhood.

I had learned about the Lenape Indians living here back in fifth grade, but I didn't realize that there were Indian burial grounds right here in Red Bank. I knew some of the American revolution had taken place near here, I didn't know it happened right here, and that it was more like a civil war for our ancestors who were colonists. I couldn't imagine going to war against a next-door neighbor or even your own brother.

I lived in New Jersey my whole life, I though slavery was just down south. Little did I know that slaves were held right here in plantations and farms all along the two rivers.

I had seen photographs of the beautiful old steamships that had once traveled the rivers. But I had no idea how important they were to the local farmers and businesses, or the important role some of them played in the American Civil War.

I had heard about Prohibition, but it really didn't make much sense to me. I had no idea that just about anyone with a boat could make a living running rum, or that speakeasys were everywhere and that bootleggers and gangsters took over local governments. I was amazed.

Just when I thought our local history couldn't get any more colorful, Mrs. Melon would bring out another amazing tale from our local history. It kind of made me proud that I live here, it's a wild and wacky place here in New Jersey.

Naturally we had to do a term paper. When we got our assigned topics, I was a bit flabbergasted. I was assigned to "choose one event or era from local history and write a paper tracing the role our local river system played in that era or event." I couldn't believe I had to concentrate on just the river!

It took me awhile to really think that through. The more I thought about it, the more sense it made. Of course, the river was important in every period of our history, and surely in many ways. But I needed to pick one specific period. I considered the American Revolution, and the era of the steamships, but settled on Prohibition. Somehow Prohibition made me laugh, I wasn't sure why. Just the idea that the government could get people to stop drinking by passing a law made me snicker. And the accounts we talked about in class about the rum runners and speakeasys were surely fascinating.

I stopped off at the library on the way home from school and picked up a few books. Kolber's, *Rise and Fall of Prohibition*, looked like a good place to start. For extra measure, I also signed out Asbury's Informal History of Prohibition. I settled in my room to read. It was going smoothly when it began again. First there came the smell, the stale cigars and a malty smell I couldn't give a name. That was followed by the murmuring again, and a faint, but weird sound. I couldn't tell what it was. Is it music? At the same time the room grew cold and I pulled my quilt up around my shoulders.

Just then Mom came home. She stopped in to be sure I had something for supper before she headed back for her second shift. She came into my room all wide eyed and demanded to know if I had been smoking. Of course, I denied it. But she persisted. When I assured her I did not smoke, she laughed and told me that then it was high time to wash my socks.

After she left I inspected the entire apartment. I couldn't smell anything at all in the kitchen or living room. There were no sounds anywhere. They could only be heard inside my room. I decided that maybe the irritation was coming up the pipes from the basement, or maybe through the walls. It didn't make any sense.

My paper was due the next week so decided I better get back to work. I was reading the chapter in Kobler's book about speakeasies. I found it astounding that there were dozens of them along our shores hidden in basements, rooftops, and secret rooms. I laughed aloud when I read that one was even uncovered in a local funeral home. It was hard to imagine what life was like back then. I guess it was then when I started to daydream.

The faint sounds of murmuring, clanging, distant voices, and that far away music slowly grew into a screeching howl. I put my hands to my ears. At the same moment, there was a loud wallop as the contents of the bookshelf flew across the room and landed in a heap. My textbooks, catcher's mitt, notebooks and papers, sweatshirts, Mom's mystery novels, and even my baby book were piled up in a lopsided mound. In the next moment, the overstuffed old photo album Mom had rescued from the hall closet soared across the room, landing on the very top of the pile.

I almost gagged when I took in a breath of foul dusty air. I stepped over to the mess and began to pick up the debris and replace it on the shelves. As I picked up the old photograph album several tattered black and white prints fluttered to the floor. I snatched them with one hand and stuffed them back inside the album. The air was suddenly ice cold. I could see my breath and I started to shiver uncontrollably.

It was then I looked up. My room had been transformed. I was standing in the middle of a different room. Well it certainly didn't look like my room, although it was about the same size. The air was filled with gray smoke that hovered over the heads of five or so men sitting at the long counter than reached across the far end of the room. The men spoke in low earnest whispers with one another. A few others, clustered in small groups, chuckled softly and seemed to be congratulating one another.

Each had a small glass into which a man perched behind the counter poured an amber liquid. As each glass was emptied it was quickly refilled. Every few minutes someone would cast a wary eye towards the door. I thought for a moment they had noticed me standing there, but they seemed to gaze right through me. No one reacted to my presence.

From somewhere music was playing, although no one seemed to be paying it any attention. Occasionally the tinkle of glassware grew loud enough to be noticed. The tall mustached man behind the bar would give the crowd a scowling look as he held up his right hand. Immediately every sound in the room ceased. Everyone sat in total silence staring at one another. In a few minutes the bar man lowered his hand and their quiet conversations resumed.

I felt a bit bolder by this time and approached the bar. Still no one seemed to notice me. I tried to speak to a man sitting on stool near me, but he ignored me. I moved closer to get a closer look.

They were all dressed in old times clothes, sort of like my grandfather might have worn. The man behind the bar had a scruffy black moustache that practically covered his face. He wore a bright bow tie on his crisp white shirt which in turn was nearly covered by a long white apron. The patrons were an assortment of sizes and shapes. Most wore suit jackets and thin ties, most of which had been loosed around their necks. Everyone was either wearing or holding a fedora or newsboy cap in his free hand.

In some ways, they looked normal. But there was something strange about them. Fat or thin, short or tall, everyone in the room was exceptionally pale skinned. They all looked like someone who had been sick a very long time and had lost all the color from their cheeks. And I noticed that I couldn't make eye contact with anyone.

I turned to look across the room when suddenly a man heading for the bar charged straight for me. His face was so close our noses nearly collided. I waited for the collision but it didn't happen. For a second I felt a brief chill pass through me. I jerked back around just in time to see the man accept a drink from the bar man.

I stood frozen there, unable to move. My thoughts were spinning around like a whirling dervish. What was going on? Then two men hopped off their stools and headed across the room to where a floor to ceiling maroon drape covered the wall. As I watched they pulled back the drape revealing a small square door hinged to the wall. They quickly opened the door and reached into the dark hole. They retrieved a wooden box containing several glass bottles. One man grabbed the box and carried it over to the bar while the other closed the small door and put the drapery back into place.

The mustached bar man grinned as he grabbed the bottles and tucked them behind the counter. Just then the door banged open crashing into the back wall. In that instant, the room grew completely silent.

The doorway was filled by an oversized man with flashing red eyes who splattered the room with oaths, curses and threats! His voice seemed to boom and echo off the walls like a thunderstorm. He stomped across the room waving a bloody hatchet at the bar man. Patrons scrambled for cover, edged under tables, and slithered into corners.

"You!" he bellowed," I got you now! You're that low life dirty bootlegger who poisoned my boy!"

"No! You got it wrong!" the bar man shouted. "You and your cheap wood grain booze. I'm gonna kill you."

"No! No! It wasn't me! I only get the real McCoy!" the bar man pleaded, "He didn't get it here.!"

With that angry man launched himself across room. Stools toppled and glass flew as he snatched the barkeeper by his collar and dragged him over the counter into the center of the room. The first punch bloodied the man's nose and ripped the tie from his neck. The bar man responded with a mighty kick to the bigger man's groin. Instantly the entire room exploded into a giant brawl. Glasses shattered, wood splintered, bodies were hurled against the walls, plaster crumbled, and the room vibrated from the countless collisions.

I scampered to my feet as soon as I could, and slowly backed away, inching my way towards the door. As I reached for the door knob I looked back one more time. The apparition had vanished. I was standing in my own bedroom again. There was no bartender, no burley man trying to kill him with a hatchet, not even the cluster of drinkers. There was no maroon curtain, no tables, or bar stools.

There was just me standing there holding the old photo album. Oh yes, there was a huge mess. My desk was tilted against the wall, two legs broken off and impaled in the opposite wall. My desk chair cushion was shredded, the bookcase was once again emptied and scattered all around the room. My bed looked like it had been trampled by a herd of cattle. But the worst of all were the walls. All along all four walls were, boot prints, smears of blood, cracks, scratches and scuffmarks, and on the wall facing the living room, a huge hole where the burley intruder had planted the hatchet.

The lights came back on the room, and instantly the radiator began to hiss. I didn't know what to do. What I did know was that my mother was going to kill me. I was shaking so badly I could hardly mover. But I had to get this room cleaned up before my mother saw it. How could I explain what had happened, when I didn't understand it myself? Who were those people? Was I going crazy?

I worked to clean up the room as best as I could. I used duct tape to fix the legs on my desk, and stuffed the ragged cushion from my desk chair into a pillow case. I cleaned up all the broken glass and debris that I could find, and set my bed back up on its frame. Then I set to work cleaning up the walls as best as I could. I washed everything off the plaster that I could, and then tried putting spackle on the smaller cracks and indentations. All I could do with the bigger holes for the time being, was to cover them with my baseball posters and some old pictures I found the front closet. Even though I was exhausted I was unable to get to sleep until well after three am.

When I went out for breakfast the next morning my mother was standing in the kitchen door way with her hands on her hips. I didn't get a chance to say a word. I had never seen my mother so angry. She demanded to know what I had been doing last night? Who had I been entertaining? Why had we been fighting?

Each time I started to describe what had happened she interrupted me, looking at me with sad eyes and shaking her head. She reminded me that we can't afford to lose this apartment, or we will be living in the car. Then she looked me right in the eye and said." I don't know what to do with you, Ted. What would your father say about this?"

I don't know if I was supposed to answer that or not. When I didn't respond, she burst into tears blubbing that she must be a terrible mother for her son to act like this. With that she bolted into her room and slammed the door. I didn't know what to do. I stood there for a minute or two, then grabbed my bookbag and headed off to school.

That afternoon when I got home from school there was a note from Mom. The note said that there was chili in the frig for my supper. At the bottom, she wrote," Please Ted, No company in the apartment to night. Please! Please!" I felt like such a jerk. I knew she was really upset. But I didn't know what to do because I didn't have any idea what had happened. I ate the chili cold and went to my room. The deadline for my term paper was in just a few days. I may as well at least try to do something right and get it finished.

I sat down at the typewriter and began to write. No matter how hard I tried to concentrate the images from last night were clogging up my brain. I had to figure out what was going on. I started to retrace the events from the previous night. I looked around my room and it looked pretty much like it had last night before the incident.

I was staring at my bookcase when I realized that this was the very counter I had seen the night before. The only difference was that the front now faced the wall. The back section was now my bookcase. With that I caught a glimpse of the bulging photograph album that Mom had rescued from the hall closet. I pulled it out and spread it out on my desk. Slowly I began to look through the photos. They were all in black and white, many were tattered and torn and were yellowed around the edges. Some images were faded so badly you could not make them out. Some of the faces seemed so familiar. I had to admit it was interesting and I wondered aloud who these people might be?

The first thing I felt was the icy cold, and then the smell of cigars. At the same moment, a faraway sound, it was music which began growing louder and louder. I jerked my eyes away from the page and looked up. It had happened again. My room was gone and I was sitting in the middle of the same smoke-filled room. There was the same long bar along the far wall, the same grayish patrons. The mustached man with the bow tie was once again pouring amber liquid into small glasses. As I stood there watching, the same man rushed towards the bar and a sudden chill once again passed right through me. Once again I watched the two men rush to the maroon drapery and return moments later with their box of liquor bottles. Then once again, the same burly man, the same cuss words, and the same bloody hatchet. It was happening again, the very same bar room brawl.

I stood there helplessly watching this rerun. What was I going to do? I must have dropped the photo album, for the next moment I was standing back in my bedroom scooping up loose photographs from the floor. The bar room, the customers, the bartender, even the burly hatchet man were gone. I looked around the room, once again there was damage everywhere. I spent hours cleaning up my room. I couldn't possibly sleep so I practiced my explanation to my mother a dozen times. But even by midnight I had no idea how to explain it to her.

I looked around the room in the morning as I dressed for school. The room looked raggedy, that's how my friends would describe it. I knew I would have to do something soon. But I didn't know where or how to begin.

As I was leaving for school I saw the super coming down the hall. I dropped head hoping he would not see me. I was wrong. His scow told me right away I was in for a lecture. That I was right about. He laced into me about the noise last night, and how he had already warned my mother once and he was sick and tired of the racket all hours of the night. He said that he should have known better than to rent to someone with a teenager. I mumbled something like," I'm sorry, but I am going to be late for school." I walked away because I didn't know what else to say.

The minute I walked in the front door that afternoon I knew right away that the super had spoken to my mother again. Mom had a look on her face I couldn't remember ever seeing before. Her entire face was a frown. I thought she might burst into tears at any moment, and yet she never made eye contact with me. I didn't know what to do or say. How could I explain what was happening when I didn't understand myself? So, I went to my room and pretended to sleep.

I didn't leave my room for anything, not even for supper. Finally, I fell asleep with the light burning and my term paper scattered all over my bed. When I awoke, it was Saturday morning. When I entered the kitchen, I could see that it was going to be a dismal day. Dark clouds covered the sky. Even the river was all brown and foamy, as if it too were angry. I didn't expect Mom to be here when I woke up, but I certainly wasn't going to ask her why she wasn't at work. She didn't speak to me when I came into the kitchen. She looked up from the sink where she was scouring with a soap pad and looked back down at her task. I grabbed a juice from the frig and went to my room.

I didn't bother getting dressed. I worked in my pajama bottoms and bare feet. Well it was now or never about the term paper, I may as well get to work. I pulled out my books, my notes and spread them across the top of the long counter and began organizing my information.

As I moved back and forth in front of the counter organizing my notecards into neat piles I stubbed my big toe on the old photo album that protruded from the bottom. The album slid from its spot dumping photographs all over the floor. Without thinking I shouted, "Dam!" and slammed my notebook on the counter.

I bent over to pick up the mess. I held the album under one arm and picked up the frayed black and white prints that had scattered across the room with the other. I stood there a moment holding a handful of pictures in my right hand and muttering to myself, or so I thought. When I looked up there in the doorway was my Mother.

She stood in the doorway with her hands on her hips, glaring at me. "Why are you cursing? "she demanded. "I want to know right now young man, what is going on?"

Mom had never shouted at me before like this. The pictures in my hand were shaking uncontrollably. I opened my mouth to answer but nothing came out. She snatched the pictures from my hand and stared at them for such a long time.

When she looked up her eyes widened and she gasped. Her hand tried to point at something, but it was shaking so badly I thought she might be having a stroke. It was at that moment I glanced around behind us. Once again, my room had disappeared. It had transformed once again into that smoke-filled bar room.

It was just as before. There was the same long bar along the far wall, with the same bartender with the giant mustache. The very same gray skinned patrons sat about in clusters drinking an amber brew from small glasses. Music played softly in the back ground, and the clinking of glassware caused the bar man to motion for quiet. As before no on paid attention to us, and once again a man rushed towards the bar and passed right through me.

Just as before no one seemed to notice us. Mom reached out and took my hand. Her face was one of horror and confusion. Then just as before the door slammed open and the burly man with the hatchet barged into the room and initiated the rowdy brawl. Again, there was smashing and crashing, cussing and fighting, and the same bloody hatchet impaled in the wall.

Mom never moved from her spot. I put my arm around her, but before I could say anything. She held up the pictures she had snatched from my hands. "Look!" she croaked, "The guy with mustache, this is a picture of him." She was right of course. Just for a moment we stared at one another before quickly inspecting the remainder of the old photos. By the time, we finished we knew that we had a photograph of "everyone "in this room.

She looked squarely into my eyes, "Ghosts!" she whispered. "They're all ghosts!" Before I could move she pulled the photo album from under my arm and shoved the photos inside.

In the next moment, Mom and I were standing back in my room. And just as before it was in shambles. There was furniture, broken and over turned, holes punched in the plaster, broken glassware, and my bed hung part way off its frame. From somewhere we heard knocking on the front door.

Mom began barking orders. "Get your stuff, pack some clothes, we are getting out of here. "And we did. We packed up our essentials and were gone before daybreak. We left just like the others. We departed in a hurry, gave no notice, and left the place in quite a mess. We left clothes, books, games, appliances, shoes, and just about anything you could imagine. Just like the others, we left rubbish; bags and bags of garbage to be cleaned out.

Gossip around town was that we were kicked out of the apartment because I was having rowdy underage booze parties. Mom had to pay the landlord so much money for the damage to the apartment, that we had to live with my grandparents for a while. Let me tell you that was no fun; rubber meatloaf every single Wednesday night! I hate meatloaf.

It wasn't until some years later, after I was out of college, that I began to research the old Twin Gables. In the archives of an old local newspaper I found an account of a man who had died of poisoned bootlegged booze at a small speakeasy, here in Red Bank. The speakeasy had been operated by a local gent in a hidden room within a building along the Navesink. It didn't give the exact address but I could tell by the description that it was Twin Gables.

A few years later I met a woman who had lived there for several years, long after we had departed. She explained that they had difficulty getting tenants to stay in that unit. One after another renters simply walked out on their leases, without notice, and inevitably left behind a big mess.

Eventually the apartment was assigned to the unmarried building superintendent. That worked for a short while, until he started a family and opened the second bedroom behind the wall closet. He too left shortly afterwards without giving notice. Over the next few years Twin Gables had a multitude of superintendents, all of which lasted only a few months.

That doesn't surprise me at all. I lived there. I have encountered those speakeasy ghosts of the Twin Gables and know them to be real. Even so, I can't help but wonder, now that the building has been torn down; have those spirits been destroyed? Did they relocate to a different portal yet to be discovered.? Or do they linger still?

Tale of Two Cemeteries: Would a Cemetery by any Other Name be as Scary?

This is the tale of two cemeteries. There is nothing particularly unique about either one. Neither is home to countless screen stars like Forrest Lawn in Hollywood. Neither is as historic as Highgate in London where countless leaders of industry, politics, and the arts, rest in peace. Fairview and Bay View cemeteries are prominent local burial grounds located here in Middletown Township, among the land of the two rivers. Admittedly there are numerous other cemeteries and church graveyards in the region, but these two hold unique tales of supernatural and unexplained events.

To fully appreciate these peculiars happening in our midst we need to be certain we are familiar with the terminology of the burial areas. Today the word cemetery is a generic term for any burial place, while in the past burial places associated with churches were called graveyards. Cemetery referred to private burial grounds, usually those with a park like setting.

But for some of us just reading the word cemetery makes us cringe. Or perhaps we inhale involuntarily when the word graveyard is used within the same sentence as "Let's go to…."? If you are like most people, you have at least an uneasiness or perhaps a mild apprehension about cemeteries.

Despite the manicured grounds, pristine landscaping, and park like appearance, would you just as soon skip that visit?

For many of us it is a simple uneasiness, a sense that you don't belong here, or that you must be careful not to walk on top of Aunt Millie. For others, the feeling is more intense. It is one of undefined anxiety as if something unforeseen and dangerous is likely to occur. Others insist that staring out across the rows of stone markers gives you the uncanny feeling that they are staring right back at you.

There are those who simply refuse to visit a burial ground, and are not about to go unless they are being carried and therefore have no voice in the matter. These individuals suffer from Coimertrophia, a fear of cemeteries. These individuals are more than uncomfortable, or merely feeling somewhat frightened. They get dizzy, sweat profusely, faint, have heart palpitations, and become nauseous. In addition, they may have bouts of excessive laughter or hysterical weeping. The number of people truly afflicted with coimertrophobia is small and you are not likely to meet up with them at Uncle Mort's funeral. These folks would simply skip the whole thing, even if they were included in Uncle Mort's will.

On the other hand, those who love visiting, talking about, and exploring cemeteries are said to be taphophiles. These individuals enjoy cemeteries. They love researching burial grounds of all kinds, examining grave markers, interpreting symbolic carvings, and making genealogical connections. Some make charcoal rubbing of unique stones, others photograph or map cemeteries, still others collect epitaphs, imagery and symbolic carvings. Most will say they enjoy the peacefulness and natural beauty of the cemetery and decry any claim they have a fetish with the dead.

Across the nation, we find a wide variety of burial grounds. There are family burial sites, private non-sectarian cemeteries, community plots, veteran burial grounds, as well as designated hospital and prison burial areas. There are also cemeteries for the indigent, usually known as potter's fields; and of course, the "country club cemetery" where the rich, famous, and infamous seek to be buried.

We all know where the local cemeteries in our area are located, we may have even been there once or twice. Yet we don't consider the sprawling grounds an integral part of our community. Yet indeed they must surely be, for as long as mankind has existed he has buried his dead. Why then are we hesitant? Why do we draw away from the cemetery?

What drives us to hold back from embracing the facility where our loved ones lie? Some psychologists would say that it is not the cemetery itself we fear, but rather death itself. Perhaps it is the trigger that forces us to face the undeniable fact, that despite our own omnipotent & narcissistic attitudes, we too are mere mortals.

We might jump to the conclusion that we get our attitudes about burial grounds from literature, movies, and television. It is certainly true that the images of walking zombies, corpses rising from graves, and mysterious murders set within a graveyard have created a general mindset that the cemetery is a scary and dangerous place. Every year at Halloween the graveyard once again becomes front and center for the mysterious, the deadly, and the unexplained.

If we look more closely at our history, we find that both oral folktales, as well as the written record have included the cemetery as the setting for countless tales and yarns of spooky and paranormal events. Even before the era of Dickens and his ghostly tales, earlier writers such as Washington Irving recounted mysterious events within the dark and dismal settings of an abandoned cemetery.

If we look farther back through the pages of history, we will see that this obsession with the dead and burial places is not at all new. Man has been burying the dead for over 100,000 years. Archeology has shown us that even the early Neanderthal man buried their dead with great care.

We know also that the ancient cultures across the globe approached death with highly individual practices, rituals, and beliefs. These were unique to their geography, culture, and religious vents. It seems obvious that despite varied locations or cultural differences they all were aware of the concept of decay and decomposition, and took care to provide appropriate disposal of human bodies.

The Greeks, Romans, and the Egyptians all had elaborate burial practices and rituals. The Egyptians are well known for their use of mummification and elaborate tombs. They built the famous pyramids and even went so far as to construct a city of the dead, an underground necropolis for disposal and appropriate burial of the deceased.

The Greeks and the Romans each had their own approaches to handling dead and disposal of the corpse. Both classic civilizations created elaborate rituals as well as tombs, grave sites, Sarcophagi, mausoleums, and utilized specific burial areas.

Here in North American the burial customs of the native Americans varied widely from one tribe to another. Some tribes left food and possessions near the gravesites, other sacrificed wives or even a favorite horse. Some blackened their faces in mourning and some wailed. A number took precautions to prevent the ghost of the deceased from returning.

Both Eastland and the Southeastern tribes were known to allow the body to decompose and then collect and save the bones for a final elaborate ritual. Mound builders buried dead in elaborate earthen tombs. Nomadic tribes often buried wherever they found soft ground or left their dead-on tree platforms. Some Southwest Indians practiced cremations, others buried dead in caves and rock fissures. Some Arctic Indians left the dead on the frozen earth for animals to devour while others buried the dead and built colorful "spirit huts" on top of the grave. There were even a few native tribes which mummified or embalmed their dead.

When the first European settlers arrived they were primarily concerned with survival. They were frankly too busy to develop an elaborate burial system. The dead were buried quickly, usually near the place of death. Frequently no markers were used to ensure that unfriendly natives did not desecrate the graves. For some years burials were random, scattered across the outer fields of the village. Even as Puritan settlements grew larger burials remained devoid of ornamentation, adhering to the Puritan ethic. During the earliest years, they refrained from establishing church graveyards fearing that such burial grounds would foster ancestor worship.

By the mid to late 1600's headstones were becoming more common, even within Puritan groups. These rounded slate tablets emphasized the Puritan belief in hell and damnation. These strikingly fearful "death head" grave markers often featured a carving of a skull with wings attached to the side of the face. In the South, there was less emphasis on hell and dammnation. Here the imagery on the stones was more angelic and emphasized the resurrection of Christ.

As America grew towns and cities became more aware of health concerns associated with dead bodies. They began creating spaces for burials on the edge of town or outside the town limits. Some of these were community grounds and other were private non-sectarian cemeteries.

This gave way in the mid 1800's to cemeteries known as memorial gardens, or memorial parks. In this era people were encouraged to spend time in these park like cemeteries. The carefully landscaped and manicured sites were exceedingly popular sites for picnics, afternoon tea, as well as visiting one's loved ones.

Throughout history there has always been class distinction regarding burials. In general, one's economic status largely determine where and how one is buried. The rich and famous usually opt for celebrity burial grounds, while the homeless and indigent may end up in a potter's field. (Potter's field derived its name from the Bible, as the burial place of the poor. It was often in an out of the way area outside the city where those making pottery would come and dig for clay for their pots.) Many church yards refused burials to suicides, criminals, or those not affiliated with that specific faith. These burials were dispersed in deserted areas of the region.

During the influx of immigrants in the 1800 and 1900's ethnic cemeteries popped up around the country. Even today many ethnic groups prefer to bury within their own cemeteries. Today anyone can be buried wherever he can afford. Rising costs have made cremation much more acceptable and is rapidly becoming a popular method of handing the deceased. Most cemeteries now offer niches for cremation urns in attractive modern columbaria.

Knowing how the cemeteries have evolved over the years may be interesting, but it still doesn't alter the fact that we have these unique and peculiar feelings about them. Moreover, we have either heard tales of the supernatural events occurring in a cemetery or perhaps we have experienced them ourselves.

One of the largest private non-sectarian cemeteries in our area is Fairview Cemetery. It is located in Middletown along Highway 35 and Chapel Hill Road in the old area which was once referred to as Hedden's Corner. It is a sprawling well-manicured park like setting with a series of paved winding lanes that intertwine throughout the immaculately landscaped property.

Established in 1851, just before the Civil War, Fairview is home to more than 21,000 graves. With several new residents arriving weekly, the cemetery provides earth burials, individual and mausoleum entombment, and niche space in its modern columbaria. From spring through autumn Fairview bursts with fresh colorful plantings, established flower beds, beautiful trees, and ornamental vegetation. It is a charming park like atmosphere.

Yet curious accounts have surfaced about this cemetery, revealing that sometimes things aren't exactly what they seem. Fairview has its share of strange, even extraordinary events.

One of the most widely reported apparitions at Fairview is known as The Victorian Lady or the Lady in White. The ghostly caller has been seen on many occasions by both staff and visitors for many years. Despite the multitude of sightings by different individuals most agree on her description. The figure is a woman of slight build with an elaborate hair style. A rope of pearls, white feathers and sprays of lily of the valley encompasses her hair which falls gently down her back.

Both her features and her clothing are stark white. She wears in an elegant Victorian gown with long lace sleeves and a high neckline. Her waist is cinched tightly, held in place by a single red rose. Her hoop skirt balloons away from her waist in great folds of sheer white fabric. She moves purposefully across the plots as if in search of something. Her movements are so graceful that she appears to be floating just inches above the ground.

Those who have seen her from afar claim that she appears to be almost transparent, and that she seems oblivious to anyone near. Others who have come upon her suddenly assert that they usually see her out of the corner of their eye. Some claim to have observed her for several minutes in this manner. But when they approach or attempt to look at her squarely in the face, she evaporates before their eyes.

Those familiar with the cemetery are accustomed to her frequent visits, and make no attempt to interfere with her meanderings in the cemetery. Whenever visitors ask staff about the strange woman in old fashioned clothes, they reply, "Oh, that is the Lady in White."

Ghost Rain

Fairview has a second highly irregular phenomena which has yet to be explained; that is the ghost rain. This manifestation has been seen literally dozens of times over the years particularly by the crews while performing their landscaping duties.

The ghost rain occurs only in the very oldest part of the cemetery over by the stand of beautiful old birch trees. It is nearly always an overcast day, but not one that threatens any kind of precipitation. As the team of workers approach the oldest section of the cemetery with their power tools and mowers they see ahead of them that it is raining. It is not just a light drizzle, it appears to be a downpour, drenching the grounds of the old section. Huge raindrops can be seen falling from the sky. Anxious not to destroy their equipment, they quickly pack up and head for shelter. If anyone rushes to the deluge area he finds the soil bone dry. This phenomenon is repeated multiple times during the summer months.

The Paupers' Field Ghost √

Until recently the State of New Jersey required that all licensed cemeteries set aside a portion of their property to provide burial for the indigent and homeless. In return the government provided a small stipend for the preparation and closing of the grave. These sad burials were seldom attended by either family or friends. Most are unmarked graves and are devoid of floral or family remembrances. The local funeral directors, under the same regulations as the cemeteries, provided minimal service for these burials. The unfortunate were buried here, without vaults, sometimes five deep, in thin particle board coffins.

Few visitors made their way to that section of the cemetery and if they did, they seldom lingered. First of all, there was an unpleasant aroma in the area, and then there was the phantom.

Both visitors and staff have witnessed a gangly old man dressed in old rags and a dirty misshaped fedora standing in Paupers' Field. The presence is known as the Pauper Field Ghost. Sometimes he simply stands in the center of the field and beckons others to come his way. Other times he is seen pacing back and forth amid the unmarked graves. His ragged clothes and unkempt appearance never changes. Crews have reported that the phantom is seen most frequently when they are mowing in the field. He moves back and forth across the plot, seemingly supervising the mowing operation. Perhaps he is insuring these graves are properly attended. Others insist that when someone does wander into the area the ragged man suddenly appears, as if providing security for the lonely outpost.

Children's Graveyard

In a secluded section of the cemetery, along Chapel Hill Road is an old children's cemetery. It is small collection of children's graves partially obscured by a small grove of dogwood trees, and small shrubbery. This area has been part of the cemetery since its earliest days with markers going back into the 1800's. They are all the graves of small children. There is no particular family, rather just a gathering of little ones resting together beneath the canopy of dogwoods overhead.

Many visitors who come upon the scene stop to stare at the collection of stones, some offering a prayer, others turn away quickly as they shake their heads. Visitors often return to these plots leaving toys, dolls, and stuffed animals. The crew has a special place in their hearts for these forlorn little graves. They check on these plots daily, often adding small plantings of flowers. Frequently they find that toys left on the graves are moved during the night to a different plot. Sometimes one or two disappear, and sometimes a new one is added overnight.

In one incident, a bright red rubber ball was left on a young boy's grave. Over a few days the staff noticed that the ball had been moved to another grave. This went on for some time. Each day the ball was on a different grave. After a while, the ball became weathered and faded. It was removed from the grave carried to the other end of the cemetery where the trash was collected. The next morning when the crew checked on the children's cemetery the ball was back in place on the boy's grave.

The Boss Snake

It is not uncommon to find wildlife roaming the cemetery. There is a wide variety of birds, rabbits, squirrels, and even a few snakes. Most are small garter snakes or the occasional black snake is sighted

But in the old section of the cemetery, and only in the older section, a peculiar "boss snake" was seen for some time. Curiously, it was only seen in the very early morning, much earlier than most heat seeking reptiles are active. This snake was peculiar as it was particularly large, being some 20 feet in length and of considerable girth.

Being abnormally large the crew decided it would be best to capture and relocate the serpent so that it didn't frighten visitors or be killed or injured by the lawn machinery. Many jokes were made about the creature among the crews, some claiming it was an apparition like some of the other manifestations they had seen in the area.

Soon afterwards two of crew caught sight of the giant reptile very early one morning. They chased the snake through the older section until they had it cornered against an old crypt. Just as they approached, one man on each side ready to grab the snake, it began to rise off the earth straight into the air. When it reached a full six feet the snake made eye contact with the two and began hissing loudly! There was no doubt the reptile was standing his ground.

The two gasped simultaneously, looked at one another, and took off at a run. They didn't stop or look back until they were well clear of the old section. When they retold their tale to the rest of the crew, their co-workers hooted in laughter. No one, however, volunteered to go catch the snake. It was decided it was best to let the boss snake alone. From then on everyone who entered the old section made lots of noise, some even sang or called out to the snake to let him know they were just passing through his domain.

Cooking A Grave.

Most of us don't give much thought about how difficult it must be to dig a grave in the winter. In our area, from November to April the ground can be frozen up to two feet from the surface. During the most frigid parts of the winters even a jack hammer can have trouble breaking through the frozen earth. But just like life, death goes on, throughout even the coldest winter. So what does the cemetery do? Well, they cook the grave.

Technology has made this an easier task than in the past, but it is by no means a simple or inexpensive process. Cemeteries use a piece of equipment known as a grave burner to heat the earth enough so that a grave can be prepared. The burner is a rectangular shaped metal appliance which is placed on the exact site of the desired grave. The device resembles a domed rectangular lid. Beneath the lid is a series of butane burners. Huge tanks of butane are connected to the burners and the apparatus operates many hours, literally roasting the earth so that it is softened. Then it must keep the soil soft until the grave can be dug. This requires that the appliance is left in place for many hours. As a result, the butane tanks supplying the energy must be replenished so that the burners do not go out; or the earth will refreeze before the grave can be dug.

This usually means that the burner is put into operation the day before the grave is dug. It is kept in operation overnight so that the soil is soft for morning. This requires that during the night watch, usually about three am, fresh butane tanks must replace the empty ones on the grave site.

This unpleasant and frigid task is done by a team of two men, who lug a new canister of butane to the grave site, and replace the old one and reconnect the burners. It isn't a job anyone ever volunteers for.

It was such a night in the middle of February that two workers left their warm beds and headed to the cemetery to make the switch of butane tanks. They came prepared wearing heavy coats, wool hats, and thick work gloves. They met at the supply shed, grabbed some lanterns, a couple of flashlights, and the huge butane tank. The tank was heavy so they loaded it on a small hand cart which they wheeled along the roadway until it ended. Then they moved along a cobblestone path until they reached the site near the grave burner. Then they hoisted the heavy canister over the frozen turf to the grave site.

They knew at once that the burner was doing its job, for the aroma of roasted chestnuts filled the air telling them the earth beneath was warm and workable. By now their hands and fingers were numb from the cold, but they swiftly disconnected the old tank and reconnected the nozzle to the new butane cylinder.

One man checked to see that the burner was lit while the other tossed the empty tank into their cart. Just then out of the icy darkness they heard a curious sound. It wasn't an animal, and there was no traffic on the highway this time of night. It took a moment before they recognized the sound, it was the dull thudding sound of a horse walking across frozen earth. They peered into the darkness of the cemetery but could see nothing.

The thud-d-thud was coming closer and with it the additional creak of an old wagon wheel. Someone was nearby with a horse and wagon. They scoured the area with their flashlights, there was nothing. They couldn't imagine who would be out on a night like this with a horse and wagon. Yet the thudding grew louder and louder. Suddenly the clatter of horses on an earthen path became the distinctive clop-clap sound of a horse and wagon moving across cobblestones. It was louder and a hollower sound than before. They recognized it immediately.

They both turned to face the commotion in the darkness. One man snatched a small flashlight, and without speaking, they raced toward the sound. They darted between the grave markers, running until they reached the cobblestone path. There was nothing there. They waited for the sound to return. But there was only the icy black air and silence, perfect silence. They shone the flash lights in every direction. The cemetery lay silent and still, blanketed in the cold and dark.

The two stood in silence for some time. They quickly gathered their equipment and hurried back to the supply shed in total silence. When they did speak, they agreed to wait until morning to tell Old Herb, the caretaker, what they had heard. Next morning when they described the event to the caretaker, he merely chuckled. He grinned and said," So, what else is new boys?"

Speaking of the Old Caretaker

Old Herb, as they called him, had worked at the cemetery as long as anyone could remember. No one knew how old he was, although he looked to be nearly a hundred, no one who worked there was about to ask. They said that many years ago, one brash young landscaper did ask Herb that very question. Herb replied," Old enough kid, and young enough to kick your ass." The young man reportedly sought employment elsewhere shortly afterwards.

Everyone liked Old Herb. He made certain that everyone did their work and did it correctly. Yet he was full of stories and enjoyed a good laugh and cold beer at the end of the shift. He lived in a small cottage in the very center of the sprawling cemetery. It was a cozy secluded spot with room for a small garden and his bird feeders. Best of all, according to Herb, was that his neighbors never threw loud parties or asked to borrow anything.

When it suited him, Old Herb shared tales of the cemetery. He described hearing the same sounds the grave burner crew had witnessed. He attributed that to the fact that the older hearses before the era of the automobile were indeed horse wagon kind of vehicles. "So, in such cases." he said," It is best to just let it be."

Old Herb also spoke of an assortment of different colored lights he frequently saw in cemetery at night. Some were orb shaped, others had a less definite form. When he first moved in there he went out nearly every night to chase away the kids he thought were causing the disturbance. He even tried chasing the colored lights with his flashlight and shotgun. But finally, he discovered there was no outside source, the lights just appeared. So he decided he would, "Just let it be."

Old Herb also told of hearing laughter throughout the grounds late at night. Occasionally, there would also be crying. Although he investigated, expecting to find intruders, the result was always the same. The laughter and the crying just appeared sometimes, its source always unknown.

As he grew older, Old Herb became very respectful of his neighbors. They didn't come visiting him at night and he did likewise. He didn't enter the cemetery at night anymore. When asked why, he responded, "When you live and work in a cemetery, you see things."

Bayview Cemetery

Bayview Cemetery is a small secluded burial ground located off Hosford Avenue in Middletown. The isolated cemetery houses 3000 graves, many of which date from the early days Monmouth County. The cemetery is set in a quiet woodland area well away from the hustle and bustle of modern day life. The gated property is open several hours each day for visitation, but closes before dusk. Curiously, unlike most burial grounds which are normally positioned at the higher elevations, the cemetery lies at the bottom of the hill.

For some years, paranormal enthusiasts have repeated accounts of curious happenings at the small cemetery in Middletown; known better to them as Greenlight Cemetery. The cemetery garnered that nickname after numerous reports of a bright green light that glimmered within the cemetery on certain nights, creating curious paranormal anomalies.

There were often disagreements about the actual origins of the strange light. Certain reports indicate that the light emanated from the cemetery itself shining light outward. Others claim that the light seemed to originate at the tree line and shone directly into the cemetery.

Accounts of these events has been published widely in our area in newspapers, magazines, and books. One Weird NJ account claims that the greenish light is that of an old caretaker who once lived near the sight. One old tale claims that he holds a greenish lantern out so that the spirits of the dead can find their way back to their graves. Still another insists that if you follow the green light, seeking its source, you will be consumed by the green forest surrounding the cemetery.

Still others claim that when the light is visible other apparitions and manifestations can also be seen and heard in the cemetery. Most accounts agree that the phenomena of the green glow is sporadic, and that one must be patient in order to see the spectral event.

According to some the greenish glow is sometimes accompanied by the apparition of a group of three small children playing among the grave markers. The three are all girls, dressed on old fashioned clothes. They appear to be singing some sort of song or rhyme which is barely audible. There are definite giggles and joyful squeals as they run about in the greenish glow. Reports insist that if the children are approached or beckoned they suddenly disappear.

Yet another account claims to have seen a woman in old fashioned widow's weeds pacing methodically through the grounds. She wears a long black dress, and a black hat with a long veil. She appears to be reading the names and inscriptions on each and every grave marker. She approaches each grave gingerly and bends over to peer at the writing carved into the stone. She shakes her head, and stands erect, and begins to wring her hands. Then she moves to the next marker and repeats the procedure. It is said that the apparition appears only when the green light is illuminating the cemetery. She will remain there for long periods of time unless she is interrupted. Should anyone approach her or call out, she vanishes.

Another account associated with the greenlight comes from several sources. Near the front gate, but off to one side are a few small weathered headstones. The markers are very old and the graves no longer receive visitors. Some visitors have claimed that when they visit the cemetery and pass by the group of small stones a small whisper is heard, "Please don't leave me." The lonely ethereal voice has beckoned callers over many years, seeking a few more moments of human contact. Interestingly one gatekeeper also reports having heard soft crying when he locks the gates for the night. It seems some of the spirits at Bayview have grown lonely.

While the claims of the green light have given the cemetery its unusual nick name, it is interesting to note that there is one report offering a rational solution to the mystery. The same Weird NJ article reports the efforts of a local man to determine the origins of the light. After investigating he asserted that the light may have emanated from the Chapel Hill lighthouse, a small lighthouse which was one of four local signals once used to mark the channel for mariners into Sandy Hook Bay. The lighthouse was taken out of service and taken down by 1995. A few years later he returned to the area and once again searched unsuccessfully for the green light.

It is unknown what has happened to the green light at Bayview. Does it still appear? And what has happened to those auxiliary manifestations? Do the children still play there? Does the widow still search the old grave markers? And do the deserted spirits still cry out in their loneliness?

Hauntings in
Middletown Village

Nestled along Kings Highway is the historic old village of Middletown. It is here where so much American history took place, and where numerous accounts of the paranormal thrive. The site is a pristine suburban thoroughfare listed in the National Register of Historic Places. The area is dotted with beautiful homes, historic buildings, old burial plots, and celebrated churches from our Colonial days.

A hundred sixty years ago, the scene was quite different. Kings Highway had grown along the junction of three former Indian paths into the widest and most heavily traveled road in the area. The small village of Middletown straddled the highway and served as the nucleus of settlement. By 1851 it consisted of about forty homes, three churches, a school, a tanner, two carriage shops, three blacksmiths, a leather and harness maker, a small boarding house, two stores, and a tavern. In addition, there were six known burial spots which included both church graveyards and private family cemeteries.

Within this historic district there is a parcel of land which has been the site of numerous exceptionally peculiar and unexplainable events as far back as the early 1850's. The tract is located along Kings Highway at the juncture of what is now New Monmouth Road. Just west of New

Monmouth Road sits the Old First Church, founded in 1688 as a Baptist church, now known as the First Church of Christ.

Just to the East on Kings Highway was the private Franklin Academy which operated beginning in 1836. When it closed in 1850 the building was turned over to the township for use as a public school. Snuggled up against the school was an old private cemetery which had fallen into somewhat disrepair.

Directly behind these two properties was an old Dutch Colonial farmhouse which faced what we now call New Monmouth Road. This property shared a low handmade rail fence that extended the entire length of the property line of both the school and the cemetery. For all appearances, it appeared that at one time it had been one piece of acreage.

There have been numerous reports of paranormal happenings in this area of Kings Highway. There also seems to be a connection between these three adjacent lots. In fact, the ghostly goings on here seem to tie the parcel of land together even more tightly than before; if that is indeed even possible.

The tale was recounted in the Daily Register in 1893 by a local who had lived in the area for some fifty years. It was considered old news, as those involved were long dead, the properties had changed hands, and no one could quite determine what had really transpired.

The family cemetery that faced Kings Highway was a private burial spot for the well-known Colonial era, Hartshorne family. Richard Hartshorne's wife, Margaret, was the first to be buried there in 1719. It was used intermittently from then until 1992 when the last burial occurred.

By 1850 there were more than two dozen grave sites here, well at least as much as one could tell. The grave markers had not weathered well in the harsh local climate. The wind and rain had washed away most of the hand chiseled images and lettering on the old brownstone markers. Many were leaning or had simply toppled over. Although someone came occasionally with a scythe and cut away the hay-like grass that grew among the stones, the cemetery had an unkempt appearance. Wild morning glories grew in the sunny spots in the spring and summer; while wild huckleberries reached out from the tree line towards the rows of stone tablets.

The fact that the cemetery was right beside the school didn't seem to bother anybody, at least no one complained. The children used the cemetery as a sort of playground. They chased one another through the rows of stones, and sometimes when the weather was hot the entire school ate their lunches while resting against the cool stone slabs. Admittedly the boys used it more often than the girls; it was the perfect place for building forts, fighting off Indians, and staging tombstone leaping contests.

Then there came a series of peculiar events in the early 1850's; phenomenon no one could quite explain. The events were discussed only in whispers at first, and then not at all. The tales didn't come to light until 1893 when the local newspaper repeated the stories.

Tragedy at the Old Dutch Farmhouse

Directly behind the school and cemetery, resting well back from the roadway was the old Dutch farm house which had been there for as long as anyone could remember. Most of the village folk didn't remember the original owners. For ten years the farm had been rented out to a farmer with a wife and young daughter. The wife died shortly after they arrived, leaving the farmer and the daughter to manage the farm themselves.

It was well known in the village that the old farmer had a fondness for the bottle. After losing his wife the problem became increasingly worse. He became what was known as a "hard drinker," as he was frequently intoxicated, and nearly always in a hostile and angry mood.

The daughter was a kind and generous eighteen-year-old girl with a warm heart that endeared her to every one of the village. She not only helped her father out on the fields, but also managed to keep the home pleasant and comfortable. No matter how difficult the old man became she made every effort to care for him in a gentle and loving way.

As time passed the old man's drinking problem became worse. He became more and more offensive and difficult to manage. By now he suffered from delirium, hallucinations, and what folks called the jim jams, uncontrollable tremors. Despite the difficulty, she tried her best to take care of him without outside help from either the church or the village.

No one really knows if he had ever been physically violent with his daughter before. But one cold and rainy night when he was very drunk, his delirium became violent. He began thrashing about the house cursing at unseen snakes and demons which he believed were stalking him. After a while he decided that the daughter had allowed the demons and snakes to enter the house and he threatened to kill her if she didn't immediately remove the invaders.

No matter what she did her father would not listen to reason. The hallucinations became worse and he grabbed a hatchet from the woodpile and began chasing his daughter throughout the house, threatening to chop her into a hundred pieces. Sometimes he would discontinue the chase just long enough to chop off the head of some unseen demon before resuming the pursuit of his daughter.

She finally managed to reach the kitchen where she shoved through the screened door and bounded across the porch onto the grass. Without slowing down, she sprinted through the vegetable garden and onto the field facing the old-school, shrieking at the top of her lungs. Her crazed father followed her screams the whole way to the school building. When she reached the school she realized that it was empty and there was no one there to help her. Exhausted and terrified she ran into the cemetery and crouched behind an old grave marker.

She could hear her father ranting and raving as he stumbled over the headstones searching for her. She huddled behind the brownstone slab hardly daring to breath. If he found her, he would surely kill her. It began to rain, a pounding cold downpour that beat down on her face as if it too wanted to punish her. She shivered and pulled herself into a ball, all the while certain he could hear her chattering teeth.

The deluge hammered the old man too, sending him staggering against a large headstone. Cursing the rain, he waved the old hatchet in the air at the offending downpour. Finally, he exhausted himself, and slowly staggered away from the cemetery and made his way home to the empty house.

It was quiet in the cemetery now. The girl was terrified still, uncertain if he had fallen asleep nearby, or perhaps he was lying in wait. So she stayed there, cowering behind the tombstone all night. After a while she fell asleep.

In the early morning, a passerby noticed her nestled against the grave maker. He called for help and she was brought to the local parsonage where she was put into a warm bed. She never regained full consciousness. The few times she appeared to be waking she merely thrashed about incoherently for a few moments and then drifted back into unconsciousness. She died two days later.

Sadly, it was some days before her father sobered up enough to realize his role in her death. Overcome with guilt and the ravages of his years of drinking, he followed his daughter to her grave a few months later.

The old house stood empty for some afterward as there were no next of kin. A few tenets took the house, but none stayed very long. They complained of mysterious crying sounds and a grotesque female apparition peeking into the windows.

Within a month, the teacher at the school left suddenly claiming that strange shadows repeatedly darkened the classroom windows. About the same time claims were made that a glowing translucent orb could be seen hovering behind one of the tombstones on dark rainy nights.

Death Shadow

Things had just begun to settle down when Jack Belcho, a young African American farm laborer reported a most peculiar event. Jack lived outside the village near the tollbooth for the Red Bank-Middletown turnpike. He had worked late that night caring for a sick horse on a farm located to the west of the village. He wasn't certain of the time as he approached the village, but assumed it must be late as there was not a single light on in any of the houses along Kings Highway. Then he heard the clock on the tavern strike midnight.

As he approached the darkened school building he heard a peculiar noise, something he couldn't identify. It was something between a gasp and squawk. He hesitated for a moment and then trudged onward, anxious to get home. Although it wasn't cold he shivered a bit and pulled his coat more tightly against his body.

He glanced at the cemetery to his left, and then back at the road ahead. There, just before him on the road was a dark object spread the width of the highway. He had stepped onto the dark spot before he realized that it was a shadow. He realized at once that it was not a normal shadow; it was exceptionally dark and threatening. Jack himself would later describe it as being "dark as coal tar."

At the same instant, his throat contracted and his neck was clutched by what felt like cold clammy fingers. An icy breath seemed to suck the air from his lungs. He raised his hands to his throat; there was nothing there. Yet he could still feel an icy compression around his windpipe.

He jerked his head to the side and glanced at the cemetery. He gurgled in horror at what he saw. Above every headstone appeared a solitary human hand, waving frantically at him, beckoning him to come that way.

It was getting harder to breath now. Jack forced in a gulp of air and looked back to the cemetery. A murky swirl of light moved to and fro among the graves throwing a peculiar greenish glow over the entire burial ground. From each headstone arose a whirling hazy cloud that morphed into a corpse right before his eyes. One after another the grotesque figures rose into the air where they hovered for a moment. Uttering a mournful wail, they vanished. From somewhere, and everywhere, Jack could hear the echo of a throng of people weeping as if there had been a great tragedy.

Jack used his last ounce of energy to thrust his body from the grip of the shadow. He staggered away from the darkness. In that instant, the grip about this throat loosened and was gone. He took a deep breath and glanced toward the cemetery. The apparition was gone! The hands, the bodies, the lights, the sounds had simply disappeared.

The cemetery looked blissfully peaceful. The tombstones, lined in neat rows, were barely visible in the moonlight. It had returned to normal. Jack turned and looked back at the peculiar shadow, and for the first time realized that the darkness took the form of a coffin lid. He took off as fast as his legs could carry him, and never looked back.

Afterwards Jack tried to recount his experience around the village to anyone who would listen. But few believed him. They all assumed that he had simply had too much to drink. But Jack knew what he had experienced, and never again walked by the cemetery at night.

Ghastly Grimace

It was less than three weeks later that the village was faced with its second mystical event. Edwin, a young man from the village, frequently spent his Sunday afternoons visiting with a farm family who lived two miles east of the village. As he always wore his best Sunday suit on these visits it was said that he was courting the farmer's young daughter. We will never know for certain if that was true. We do know that he visited frequently, and was apparently always welcomed by his hosts.

On this particular evening, Edwin stayed much later than he had intended. It was well after dark when he made his goodbyes and headed back to the village. Soon after leaving the farmhouse he noticed that not only had the moon become veiled by thick dark clouds; but now the wind had awoken in a frenzy. Blasts of damp ocean air stung his face. The farther he traveled the worse it became until the wind was nearly pushing him backwards. Edwin knew that storm was imminent. He picked up his pace, as much as his stiff leather Sunday shoes would allow, and hurried on towards home.

He was about a hundred yards from the cemetery when the thunder boomed, lightning flashed, and the skies opened. Rain fell in torrents, obscuring his view. There was no shelter at the cemetery so he made a dash for the darkened school building. To his relief, he discovered that the front door was unlocked. At least he would not ruin his suit.

He let himself inside and shook the water off his coat. A small window on each side of the room allowed fragments of light into the tiny vestibule. In the center of the entranceway was a bell tower. A long rope dangled from the small bell suspended at the very top. On each side a flight of stairs reached to a second floor.

Edwin felt his way along the outer wall to the downstairs classroom door. It was locked. Another bolt of lightning gave Edwin just enough light to find his way to the staircase. In the darkness, he carefully climbed the stairs one step at a time. When he reached the landing on the second floor he discovered that this time the classroom door was open.

Outside the storm roared. Thunder rumbled and crashed. Streaks of yellow and green lightning illuminated the sky in an eerie glow which lasted only a few seconds, before plunging the landscape into total darkness once again.

Just as he stepped into the room another bright bolt illuminated the room. He quickly scanned the room. The children's' desks were lined in neat rows with a large wooden teacher's desk at the front. In front of her desk was the recitation bench. It was along narrow bench on which small groups of children would attend their lessons with their teacher, and verbally recite what they had just learned.

Edwin carefully made his way in the dark through the rows of chairs to the bench. He folded his coat neatly and laid it on the far edge of the bench. Using it as his pillow, he stretched out full length. At least he could rest until the storm blew over.

He wasn't certain how long he had slept before a particularly loud clash of thunder woke him. Just then he heard a woman scream. Before he could reach the window there was a second scream. The next unyielding shriek of agony seemed to penetrate through his body right to his bones.

He pressed his face against the window pane. At first, he didn't see anything. Then there was another flash of lightning and there on the other side of the pane of glass was the grisly face of a woman. The expressionless cloudy eyes stared into his. The skin had been stripped away from the remainder of the face leaving a few facial bones protruding though the mass of rotting flesh. All the tissue around the mouth was gone so that the teeth were fully exposed creating a horrifying grimace.

The darkness returned leaving Edwin shaking uncontrollably. He told himself that he had just imagined it and turned away from the window to sit on the bench. Then he heard a tapping sound on the window. He listened for a moment, the tapping stopped. In a few minutes, it started again, tapping first on one window pane and then moving on to the next. Each time the sound grew a bit louder than the one before.

Edwin was breathing heavily when he mustered the courage to look out the window once more. In the darkness, he could see nothing except the sheets of rain that splattered off the windows in great gushes. There was another flash of lighting and for a moment Edwin could see the entire school yard illuminated in a dim yellow light. There was no one there.

As he turned away from the window he heard the front door of the schoolhouse slam open. At first, he scolded himself for not securing it more tightly. Then he heard the footsteps. They were heavy and arduous steps, moving methodically around the locked classroom below. Edwin caught his breath and told himself it must be another traveler seeking shelter from the storm. How did he get into the locked classroom?

It was quiet for what seemed a very long time before he heard the first deliberate steps on the staircase. The hair stood up on the back of his neck at the very moment his entire body turned icy cold. Ever so slowly, cautiously, and purposefully someone climbed the stairs. Edwin called out, "Who's there?" No one answered. There was a thud as someone or something reached the top step. It was followed by a crash as it collided with the classroom door. Edwin heard the latch release and the squeak of the hinges as the door swung opened.

At that moment, another bolt of lightning filled the room with light and the apparition greeted him with a ghastly grimace. It was the same mutilated face he had seen in the windows panes. Now in the darkness the form took on its own peculiar bile colored glow. The woman never took her eyes off Edwin. The face was as before, a partially defleshed cranium, with exposed teeth forced into a most hideous grin. Long tangled masses of hair hung down on her shoulders partially covering her stained and mildewed funeral shroud. Skeletal hands reached out from beneath the layers of fabric as if to embrace him. She staggered towards him whispering his name.

Edwin bellowed something unintelligible as he tore past the grotesque creature. He bolted out the door onto the landing before jumping from the top step. He landed half way down smashing his ankle against the wall. The searing pain took his breath away for a moment, but he had no time to lose. He pulled himself up and took off running, out the front door of the school into the school yard. Looking over his shoulder he saw to his horror that the hideous creature was in pursuit.

He was half way through the cemetery when he realized his mistake, for the instant the hideous creature reached the boundary of the cemetery she shrieked in glee with a great cackle. Edwin spun to the right and darted back onto Kings Highway. He ran towards the village nearly hysterical with fear.

When he came to the first house in the village he charged straight into the door without stopping. The lock gave way, Edwin tumbled into the house striking his head on the edge of a table. When he awoke, he was in bed and a doctor stood over him nodding disapprovingly.

Edwin was bed ridden for several weeks and even afterwards was prone to fits of anxiety and nervousness. He was never able to go back to work, and would never again visit the farmer's daughter. Shortly after the new year he passed away. As Edwin's story spread, most people insisted that his delusions were due to his serious injury and fright.

The events of that year were the talk of the village for a while. Many dismissed the series of events as old wife's tale. A few discussed it openly as a paranormal experience; while others spoke of it behind closed doors, and only in whispers.

Just as we cannot deny those parts of written history simply because we do not like or understand them, so then how do we deny these accounts of the supernatural, archived by our ancestors.? After all, these most peculiar events are a part of the heritage and deliciously rich history that is Middletown Village.

The Guyon Point Phantom

G uyon Point, located on the northern shore line of the Navesink, lies just off Navesink River Road in Middletown. Nearly opposite Fair Haven's Lewis Point, Guyon Point juts into the river providing panoramic views of the river and southern shoreline. The Point is named for James Guyon Timolat, whose opulent summer estate, the Riverside, once encompassed the entire Point. Although no longer one single estate, the Point remains an elite neighborhood of impressive residences.

For decades' numerous accounts of peculiar events at the site have circulated around the riverfront. One legend shared by multiple witnesses describes the occasional sighting of an empty weathered rowboat found just off Guyon Point. Witnesses claim to have seen an aged rowboat floating aimlessly in the early morning, just as the fog is lifting from the water. A hunched-over old man grasps the side of the old boat as he peers intently into the water. He seems to be calling out, although not a sound can be heard. If approached by another craft, the apparition disappears. Several witnesses insist that the specter is a grandfather from the mid 1900's who lost his grandson in a fishing accident many years ago.

Ernest had lived and worked on the river his entire life. So, when he reached middle age he was delighted when he secured a job as the caretaker for the massive estate on Guyon Point. The grounds were huge and there was always something to do. But he didn't mind. The owners frequently travelled and were usually gone the entire winter. Ernest maintained the grounds, did odd carpentry, and kept fires in the big house to ward off the damp during their absence.

Ernest often said the best part of the job was the little cottage on the estate which came with the job. With his children grown, it was perfect for him and his wife. They loved the tidy clapboard bungalow located some distance from the manor house on a small cove on the river.

Even after many years he never lost his love of the river, nor his respect for its power. Every summer his grandson came to visit for several weeks. They spent many happy hours fishing and crabbing along the shore of Navesink. The young boy constantly begged his grandfather to take him out in the boat so they could catch, "a really big fish." The grandfather told his grandson, Paul, that only when he had learned to swim, would they go off Guyon Point into the deeper water.

"But I just want to fish," the boy pestered.

"When you can swim young man, not until then," was the unchanging reply.

The year he was about to turn six the boy arrived with exciting news. He told his grandparents that he had finally learned to swim. He described in detail the swimming lessons, and demonstrated with his arms the different swim strokes he had mastered.

True to his word the very next day his grandfather dragged the old rowboat down to the river bank. The two loaded up their fishing tackle, a jar of clam worms and set out across the channel. They rowed to a spot just off Guyon Point, where the water was known to be particularly deep. The boy was determined that they would catch a snapper or a striped bass for their supper.

They cast their lines into the deep water and waited. In a moment or two something tugged on the boy's line bending his pole toward the surface of the water. The boy grabbed the pole with both hands as his grandfather shouted to him to set the hook by jerking the pole upward. The boy grunted has he yanked his pole skyward.

"Now start reeling it in," his grandfather called. It took all the boy's strength to hold onto the pole with one hand and at the same time turn the crank on the reel. After what seemed like a lengthy struggle a giant silver sliver flashed above the water.

The boy screeched," Look! I caught…" Just for a moment his grip loosened on the pole. He saw his mistake in an instant, but it was too late. The great fish dove to the bottom yanking the boy over the side of the boat into the water with a great splash.

Ernest reached out to grab the boy but caught only some briny spray. Expecting the boy to pop to the surface the grandfather chuckled as he peered at the water. But then there was nothing. There was no flailing, or splashing, not even a bubble. Ernest shouted out the boy's name. He yanked off his shoes and dove into to the water. He dove as deeply as he could, but saw no sign of his grandson. He kept returning to the surface for air and then dove again into the depths. The water was deep here and he could not reach the bottom. The commotion alerted other fishermen who came to his aid. But there was no sign of the boy. The body of the boy was never found.

Now it is reported that on certain mornings, just as the fog is lifting off the water, the apparition of the rowboat can be seen off Guyon Point. A frantic grandfather still searches in vain for his lost grandson. As soon as the sun is bright, the apparition disappears.

Records from the investigation of the incident reveal that the boy had fibbed to his grandfather, he had not learned to swim at all. He just wanted to go fishing.

The Woman In Black

For those that can remember, the 1960's were, as Charles Dickens wrote in the opening to A Tale of Two Cities, "The best of times, it was the worst of times, it was the age of wisdom, it was the age of foolishness, it was the epoch of belief, it was the epoch of incredulity, it was the season of Light, it was the season of Darkness............"

The decade began as the youngest man ever elected to the presidency moved into the White house with his young wife and small children. Man walked on the moon for the first time, Martin Luther King led non-violent protests for civil rights, and the pill became readily available for the first time. As color televisions began filling American homes, the first ever super bowl was televised across the nation. Johnny Carson popularized the Tonight Show, the Beatles appeared on the Ed Sullivan Show, and the nightly news carried the horrific scenes of war from Vietnam, further dividing the American public.

Before the decade had ended both the young president and Martin Luther King would be assassinated. There would be violent antiwar protests, anti-civil rights atrocities, a cold war with Russia, and an international fear of nuclear obliteration.

On the home front the 1960's brought on a major change in American fashion. The mini skirt appeared in 1965 followed by tie dye tee shirts, jeans as a principal attire, and an overall diverse approach to fashion that the young embraced and the old folks abhorred. These were the days of Andy Warhol's Campbell Soup can, VW bugs painted in rainbows, and psychedelic everything. It was also the era when marihuana was called grass, when fathers shouted at their sons about their long hair, and of a legendary music festival called Woodstock.

Red Bank prospered during the sixties, storefronts were filled with the latest fashions, home goods, and technologies of the day. People still shopped on Friday nights and Saturday. Broad Street hummed with the sounds of jingling cash registers, shoppers, and of high powered car engines.

No one could recall exactly when she first appeared. By the time her reoccurring presence was noted it was agreed she had been there for several months. A beautiful young woman arrived early every Saturday morning on Broad Street and then spent the day walking slowly up and down both sides of the street.

She was an attractive young woman dressed in the latest British "mod" fashion. She appeared at first as if she were a fashion model straight out of Great Britain. Her makeup was immaculate, and her black leather outfit was upscale and chic. It was perfectly coordinated with her tall leather boots, dark beret and oversized sun glasses.

At first people thought she was a model hired by local clothing stores to advertise their latest inventory. Others insisted she was a college student home for the weekend, still others were certain she was a British au pair or perhaps a nanny from a nearby estate.

She neither spoke or made eye contact with anyone. Her face remained expressionless, never smiling or frowning. Each Saturday her routine was the same. She just appeared and sauntered up and down Broad Street. She never entered any stores or businesses, and was never seen stopping for food or visiting a rest room. For a long time, people simply ignored her.

After a while people noticed the change in her appearance. Ever so slowly her trendy outfit gave way to dark ill-fitting and rather shabby clothing. Her feet, no longer in fashionable boots, dragged along the pavement in bulky clogs making a scraping sound as she passed. The black leather was gone, replaced with an unkempt black cape over a long black dress. Her once immaculate fingernails nails were smeared with a black nail polish. Her hair grew longer and longer until it trailed off her back like a mane. What could be seen of her face took on a grayish cast which developed into a definite violet hue. About the same time her lips slowly shriveled into thin serpentine lines. In fact, her entire body seemed to shrink until she was just a shell within the baggy folds of her dark garb. Her gait slowed noticeably, but her pace remained steady and determined.

Despite Red Bank's small size no one knew her name or where she lived. No matter who you asked, no one could recall having ever seen her before anywhere in town. To make matters even more bizarre, no one ever saw her arrive on Broad Street. She didn't seem to drive a car, nor did anyone seem to drop her off. She would just suddenly appear early each Saturday regardless of the weather. Neither rain, snow, wind, nor'easter deterred her. She suddenly appeared every Saturday morning and began her long lonely march.

It wasn't long before adults and children alike stared openly at her. Young children gawked and sometimes broke into tears believing she was a witch. They clutched their mothers when they passed her on the street and often pointed a tiny finger her direction. If she ever noticed, she never responded. Older and braver youngsters attempted to talk with her without success. She ignored anyone who greeted her or attempted to stop her in the street. Even when teenagers taunted her, she remained silent. When approached by well-meaning adults who offered her shelter during a storm she hurried away without speaking. She refused to make eye contact with anyone.

People sometimes stopped on street corners in small groups and discussed the unusual woman. There was a litany of speculation about the woman in black. There were two schools of thought, one who believed her to be mortal and another who deemed her to be an apparition of some sort.

One group said she was a teen who had turned to drugs, and as her addiction worsened so did her appearance and behavior. Their supposition was that she wandered in a drug induced haze. Others claim that she was most certainly the child of a well-known local mental patient who had committed suicide few years earlier, abandoning the five-year-old child. They believed her wanderings were attempts to find her deceased mother.

Still another claim was that she had lived in Red Bank as a youngster. But she was a peculiar girl who was sent away by her parents. They declared she was deeply disturbed and merely trying to find her childhood home.

Still others had a more contemporary explanation. This group insisted that she was engaged to a young man who was drafted and sent to Vietnam. When he failed to return home, she took on this silent vigil as a protest of the draft system and the ongoing war.

There was a sizeable group who had a more paranormal approach to the case. Since witchcraft had flourished in the 60's there was a contingent that believed she was indeed a witch. Although they didn't explain why she kept up her lengthy vigil in Red Bank.

There were several groups which felt she was most certainly the specter of a young wife who had spent many years searching for her lost husband. In one version, he was run over by a horse and carriage on Broad Street many years before, and so disfigured she could not recognize him. She didn't believe the dead man could be her husband and so she searched on for him. Another said her husband died in a fire on Broad street and she searched for his remains. Another that he was a soldier lost in the second world war. Yet others claim that he was a drunk and a womanizer who had simply left her, and that she was spending eternity trying to bring him back home.

Still others believed her to be a supernatural spirit insisting that she was a warning specter from mother earth. They believed that nuclear war was imminent and that the mother earth specter was in mourning for the coming end of civilization. A similar theory was that the very act of the young woman morphing into the old crone was merely a premonition of mankind's coming extinction. Despite all these theories, no evidence has ever been discovered to support any of the many explanations of the lady in black.

One Saturday just before the new decade began she simply failed to arrive. She was never seen again. We may never know the name of the silent figure in black who patrolled Broad Street in the midst of the 60's, or even if she was a spectral or physical being. Perhaps it is just as well.

Allowing Red Bank's lady in black to remain anonymous and thus shelter her personal secret may leave us seeking closure. But perhaps it is a kindness we need to offer this unknown lady or should I say, nameless specter. You decide.

The Bad Luck Boys
The Unfortunate Demise and Spectral Sightings of the Great Explorers.

Do you remember sitting on that hard-wooden chair in an elementary school classroom listening as your teacher described the adventures of the great European explorers such as Magellan, Hudson, Columbus, and Sir Walter Raleigh? Did you tend to do a bit of daydreaming? Most of us did. Or perhaps you fantasized you were a famous explorer with a ship of your own. Or maybe you circumnavigated the earth to return to a hero's welcome; or possibly found new lands which they named for you. Perhaps you imagined you were a member of Henry Hudson's crew as he explored the local shores of Sandy Hook Bay or met with the Leni Lenape at the mouth of our rivers along shore of the Highlands.

Of course, this probably occurred before the teacher told you that you were required to memorize names, dates, and places, and which of the many kings of Europe sponsored each and every voyage. At that point your enthusiasm for their exploits may have dwindled significantly. If that was agonizing for you, and if you are the slightest bit passive aggressive, you may be pleased to learn that many of the famous explorers either vanished off the face of the earth, or met an untimely or gruesome death. In addition, it seems that for some enigmatic reason, the spirits of these adventurers have not been allowed to rest in peace. Specters, hauntings, and apparitions of these unfortunate souls have been witnessed across the globe for centuries.

Among those who simply vanished without a trace was an expedition from Portugal with brothers, Gaspar and Miguel Corte-Real. While on an ocean voyage in 1502 they simply vanished. Ever since, the inhabitants of their small coastal hometown claim to be able to predict the arrival of severe marine storms. Just before the onset of such a gale they claim the manifestation of the two brothers, wrestling in vain with canvas sails aboard an ancient sailing ship, is seen just north of the harbor.

A similar event occurred in 1864 when adventurer, John Franklin and Francis Crozier, disappeared in the Arctic. Neither their ship or the remains of the two have ever been discovered. It has been assumed that their ship became trapped in the ice and they perished. Yet no wreckage or bodies have ever been discovered. Inuit folklore insists that visions of the ship appear frequently just before a blizzard.

A British explorer, Perry Fawcett, vanished in the Amazon in 1925 while searching for a mythical city in the jungle. A few accounts from an Amazonian tribe, the Akuntsu, claim to see a pale skinned man appear just before the coming of danger or a tragedy for the tribe. The ragged and disheveled fair haired man stands silently just outside the camp gaping at the cooking food. If approached, he vanishes. As recent as the 1980's, the tribe reported the specter to some Christian missionaries in the area. Shortly afterwards Brazilian ranchers massacred the entire population of the Akuntsu, except for three individuals.

Half way around the world, off the southern most coast of Australia, lies the Bass strait. This narrow body of water separates Australia from the island of Tanzania. It was here in 1803 that explorer, George Bass vanished without a trace. A surgeon turned explorer, and entrepreneur, Bass was well known in the Melbourne area. One day Bass headed across the strait to Tanzania. He never arrived and no wreckage was ever spotted. A few old-time mariners claim that his ghost appears sometimes, mostly on cloudy nights plodding slowly through churning waters of the strait.

In case you think this occurred only in the distance past, consider the case of Peng Jiamu. In 1980 a Chinese biochemist, Jiami was leading a scientific expedition in the desert near Lop Nor, China. He excused himself from the group saying he was going for a drink of water, and vanished without a trace. Despite a massive search by the Chinse government, not a trace, not even a skeleton was ever found. Few of the nomads of the area are willing to speak of the disappearance. Those who will, claim that on certain moonless nights his ghost is seen moving across the desert, not really walking, rather floating some two feet above the surface of the barren desert floor.

The list of adventurers and exploders who vanished is quite lengthy. Of course, vanishing without a trace could have reasonable explanations. Ships can sink, and individuals face countless hazards when travelling in the wilderness. They can be killed and eaten by wild animals, fall prey to natural disasters, have accidents, ingest poisons, become ill, face starvation, or simply become lost. Yet we must admit the accounts of these events are quite striking, as are the historical records of their subsequent spectral sightings.

Likewise, the peculiar and sometime tragic demise of many of the famous New World explorers is singularly perplexing. Christopher Columbus never knew he had discovered the New World. He was merely trying to find a passage to Asia. After his voyages, Columbus lost favor with the court as he became increasingly mentally unbalanced. As his behavior become more and more unpredictable Columbus was excluded from Court, society, and most of his family. Columbus died at the age of 55, a broken, depressed, and lonely man.

Over the centuries numerous accounts of spectral images of the explorer have been claimed. Several sites near Huelva, Spain lay claim to the navigator. The most significant, however, is at the chapel of *Sanctuario de Neustra Senora de la Cinta* just a mile outside of Huelva. The fifteen-century chapel holds a statue of Columbus's patron saint, Virgen de la Cinta, as well as a relic of the saint, which Columbus is reported to have carried with him on his voyages. Columbus never failed to stop at the chapel to venerate the saint before he left on an expedition. Today the site is a tourist destination where visitors often claim to glimpse a manifestation of Columbus kneeling before the statue of the saint.

When Portuguese explorer, Vasco da Gama, successfully found a passage to India he returned home a national hero. As a reward, he was appointed Viceroy of India in 1524. Within days, before he could accept the appointment, he had died of malaria. It was more than a month later that his flagship the *Sao Gabriel* limped back into Lisbon, heavily damaged and leaking badly. According to legend, specters of the damaged and leaking ship often appear at the entry to Port Lisbon, as if waiting for its captain to bring her into harbor.

The Spanish explorer, Balboa was the first to see the Pacific Ocean and claim it for Spain. He also established settlements on the Isthmus of Panama as well as on the South American continent. Although he returned home a hero, he was beheaded in 1518 for treason. Claims have been made both in Spain as well as in his settlement of Darien in South America that the headless ghost of Balboa has been seen roaming the streets, perhaps in search of his own cranium.

Perhaps one of the most famous explorers of the era was Ferdinand Magellan who was first to cross the Pacific. Although his expedition successfully circumnavigated the globe, Magellan himself did not live to see the celebration. He was killed during a skirmish in the Philippines. Some accounts say it was a machete wound, others claim it was a poison arrow. At the time of his death his flag ship the *Trinidad* was scuttled nearby. Reports have circulated for centuries that the *Trinidad* appears near the location of Magellan's death, waiting silently for the return of its captain.

Captain James Cook, English explorer and cartographer, mapped large areas of the Pacific. On his fourth voyage, he stopped in the Hawaiian Islands for supplies. There he got into a dispute with the local tribal chief. When Cook tried to kidnap the chief and hold him for ransom a local mob turned on the explorer and hacked him to death. Locals insist that on the date of the insurrection, February 14th, the apparition of Cook running for his life from a howling mob can be seen along the waterfront, just as the sun is about to rise.

Sir Walter Raleigh, an English adventurer, is best known in America as the founder of the Roanoke settlement in Virginia. He is remembered as the gallant knight whospread his cape across a puddle so that Queen Elizabeth I would not get her shoes dirty. He was in fact such a favorite of the Queen that when he married one of her ladies in waiting without the Queen's permission, the Queen was so enraged that she issued a death warrant and had the couple locked in the tower of London for twelve years. Apparently, Elizabeth didn't have the heart to carry out the execution.

After her death, her successor, James I, had the explorer beheaded at the Tower in Westminster. It is well known that the Tower of London has boasted many a specter, phantom, and unseen spirit, not to mention full body apparitions. So, it is not surprising that there have been numerous sightings of the gentlemen knight dressed in elaborate Elizabethan attire roaming the halls of the Tower.

While these explorers played an important role in the discovery of the New World, there are two who are better known to us. Anyone who grew up here or have lived here very long is familiar with Henry Hudson and Giovanni Verrazano. We find their names on schools, parks, streets, bridges, and even municipalities across our region. Who has not heard of Henry Hudson High School, Hudson County, and of course the Verrazano Narrows Bridge?

Until the sixteenth century the Jersey Shore and her the twin rivers; the Navesink and Shrewsbury were the domain of native Americans known as Leni Lenape. At the beginning of the century an old Lenape soothsayer named Cokokua predicted that very soon a great canoe would come from across the water bearing men without color. He warned the native Americans to beware of these men; for they would bring destruction to the Lenape people. Indeed, his prediction would come true. By the late 1700's the Lenape had been scattered far and wide from their original homes along the Navesink and Shrewsbury rivers.

This first sighting of the pale skinned Europeans came in 1524 when an Italian explorer, Giovanni Verrazano first surveyed the area. Like many others, he was searching for a passage to India. During this voyage he charted the Eastern coast of America from the Carolinas to Newfoundland. From the detailed diary of his journey we know that he was unimpressed with the sandy beaches of the Jersey shore, considering them to be a hindrance to shipping. Verrazano never stepped foot on our soil, but did inhabit the lower tip of Manhattan while waiting out a storm. He also recorded that on July 8, 1524 while passing our shores the Lenape demonstrated great "impertinence" to his expedition. As the ship passed a group of Lenape on shore turned their backs and pushed their buttocks outward toward the crew as a sign of contempt.

After leaving our shores that summer of 1524 Verrazano sailed northward along the coast. He encountered native Americans near modern day Rhode Island. The natives were hospitable to the strangers, even guiding his gale torn ship, the Delfina, into safe anchorage in what is now Newport Harbor. When Verrazano sailed away from the harbor he had a fresh supply of food and water and two native American children he had kidnapped. Although he reportedly left with two young boys only one would survive the trip. Upon reaching the Old World he sold the youngster to a marketer who put the child on display as a traveling side show.

During his final voyage in 1528, Verrazano explored the coast of Florida and the Caribbean. Having just passed Jamaica he sailed south east for several days until he came to a small lush island which he believed to be uninhabited. When Verrazano and a handful of his crew landed on the beach they were promptly killed and eaten by cannibals. The remainder of the crew could only watch in horror from the safety of the ship. They quickly sailed away when the natives took to their canoes.

It isn't surprising that there have been numerous claims of spectral sightings of Verrazano. Like so many of the other explorers of that era Verrazano and his crew behaved abdominally toward the native Americans. Looting, theft, kidnapping, rape, and murder were the norm (Ships of nearly every European power participated in these duplicitous interactions with local populations.)

It is not at all surprising that all this negative energy has remained here; sometimes latent, and other times active and observable. Spectral beings tend to have a geography, that is they tend to stay at the place of their agony or demise. So, it is not surprising that the accounts of spectral activity involving Verrazano occur all along the Eastern Coast of the United States

Numerous accounts are reported from the New England Coast, particularly in the Rhode Island region. It was from these shores that Verrazano kidnaped the native American children. Over the years, multiple accounts claim to hear children crying in great distress near the shoreline. Another account of this same incident goes further, reporting seeing the specter of two young native American boys cowering in fear as two sneering sailors approach them. The apparition is observed close to the anniversary of the abduction.

Another outbreak of peculiar events centers around the Jamestown

Verrazano Bridge, the four-lane, mile and half long concrete bridge that spans Narragansett Bay connecting North Kingstown with Jamestown. Since its completion in 1992 the bridge has been plagued with multiple problems including structural glitches as well as the ongoing challenge of suicide attempts. Special services report to the bridge nearly a dozen times each year in an attempt to rescue jumpers from the bridge deck. They are not always successful.

Mariners complain that when sailing under the bridge at night they are sometimes accosted by a large wake from some unseen vessel. The effect disrupts the navigation routes of large ships and is more severe on smaller vessels causing them to be nearly swamped. So many complaints have reached the Coast Guard that radar monitoring of the area is carried out in the vicinity of the bridge. There are no images visible on the radar during the times when boaters claim being attacked by the monstrous wake.

The Verrazano Narrows Bridge in New York marks the gateway to New York harbor. Stretching 13,700 feet across the Hudson, the twelve-lane bridge separates the bay from the river. Opened in 1964 the bridge connects Staten Island with Brooklyn. More than 200,000 vehicles cross the span daily making it one of the busiest commuter crossings in the country. The bridge stands 228 feet above the water's surface to allow the great ocean liners, tankers, and container vessels access to the harbor. This height required the bridge's vertical uprights to be seventy stories tall and especially adapted to compensate for the curvature of the earth.

Since its inception, the bridge has been plagued with difficulty. Three men died during the construction, political wrangling delayed the project, and even once completed there was a dispute over its name. Like the Jamestown Verrazano the span quickly developed a reputation as a common choice for attempted suicides.

Another report is of peculiar lights emanating from beneath bridge on certain nights. These lights appear to change shapes and create forms resembling people, ships, and even navigational markers These peculiar lights beckon the unwary mariner, leading them from the safety of the channel into the shoals where they can be stranded. They appear in a series of colors from pale white to a greenish yellow, and have even caused commercial ships to veer from their course dangerously close to other ships or shallows.

Another paranormal account centers around the collision of the *Sea Witch,* a 610-foot container vessel and the 700-foot-long *Brussels,* an Esso oil tanker. As the two ships were passing beneath the bridge on June 1, 1973 the *Sea Witch* unsuccessfully attempted to make some course corrections resulting in a collision with the *Brussels.* The two vessels were interlocked when fire erupted scorching the deck of the bridge and incinerating both vessels. It was only when the anchor of the Brussels gave way that the tide carried the ships downstream preventing catastrophic damage to the bridge. Eventually the fire was extinguished and the tide carried the two ruined hulls into Gravesend Bay.

Witnesses claim that if you cruise beneath the bridge about 12:20am on June 1st you will hear the death cries of the sixteen sailors who died in the inferno. The same witnesses claim to feel intense heat, and smell the rancid aroma of burning oil. Although we cannot directly attribute these to Verrazano himself, we can consider that the intense negative energy created by his visit to these shores may be lingering still near the bridge that bears his name.

If one believes in Karma, we might say that Verrazano met his just rewards by his manner of death. Being hacked to death and then cooked and eaten certainly has a ring of payback. None the less, it isn't surprising that in Guadalupe, a small lush island in the Caribbean, local folklore tells of a singularly extraordinary manifestation. The apparition appears only once a year, in mid-October, the anniversary of this death, in a small cove on the Northeast coast.

The account is by an elderly local, Jean-Louis, who listened to the accounts of the event at his grandmother's knee. Although he had begged his mother to take him to the spot to see where it happened, she adamantly refused, and forbade him from ever venturing to the small bay on the Northeast coastline. It wasn't until a few years ago he decided to visit the secluded cove himself, on the anniversary of the incident. The *fete patreonale* had been celebrated just a few days before, and Jean Louis was in an adventuresome mood, still feeling the effects of the celebration.

On that night in mid-October Jean-Louis waited until dark before heading down the path that lead from the village to the shoreline. A gentle sea breeze rustled thru the palms and the sound of peepers and the chatter of the nighttime insects surrounded him as he moved farther away from the village. As he moved closer to the beach he noticed an acrid aroma in the air. He paused, it was an odor he had never smelled before. It didn't seem to belong here on the beach.

When he reached the shoreline Jean-Louis leaned against a palm and gazed out across the cove. The white sands and the gentle splashing surf reflected in the moonlight creating a scene of peace and tranquility. He slid down along the trunk of the tree and sat down to rest in the sand.

He couldn't remember how long he sat there, or how he first became aware of the peculiar smell. He was once again aware of the acrid smell, it was more of a stench really, and it didn't seem to belong here on the beach. No one was cooking nearby and he wondered aloud where the smell was coming from.

That is when he saw it. Just off shore he saw a handful of grayish blobs hovering in the shallow water. They moved resolutely toward the beach. As they drew closer Jean-Louis could make out that they appeared to be sailors. They were very grayish indeed and they wore old fashioned mariners' togs, doublets with loose trousers and wore small knit hats. The leader of the group wore neater clothes which were more fitted to his body. He carried a saber on his side and wore a long curly beard.

Jean Louis rubbed his eyes in disbelief. The line of phantoms moved across the beach toward the tree line. He called out to the group but there was no response. At that moment, there was a shriek from the jungle and a throng of natives sprang from the underbrush. Before the sailors could respond the group was upon them. The leader attempted to flee back into the water but was quickly caught and decapitated on the spot. As Jean Loui watched in horror, the sailors were hacked to death. The screams of the victims echoed across the bay, and blood teemed into the crystal clear Caribbean waters. Jean-Louis began to shake uncontrollably. Immediately he was nauseated by the stench of the blood and sight of the body parts scattered across the beach.

As he watched, a group of the natives built a large fire on the beach while the others gathered the scattered body parts. Laughing and singing they roasted the assorted body parts over the fire. That faint stench he had noticed earlier was now overpowering, it wasn't exactly like lamb cooking, more like a smoked pork. Jean-Louis realized he was smelling the aroma of cooked human flesh and he turned his head aside and retched.

He barely had time to recover when he caught a movement out of the corner of his eye. He caught his breath, there stood one of the natives holding a piece of barbequed foot in one hand. He grinned with dancing eyes, and extended his arm offering the cooked foot to Jean- Louis.

Without saying so much as "No, thank you," Jean-Louis ran from the beach as fast as his legs could carry him. He never looked back and did not slow down until he reached the center of the village. There he collapsed in exhaustion. When he awoke, it was daylight, and two of the elder women of the village stood over him making rude remarks about his drunkenness and lack of self-respect. Jean-Louis did not share his adventure with anyone for a very long time.

It is evident that although Verrazano did not step foot on our beaches, or explore our river system, the after-effects of his visit linger still; both here near "his bridge," in New England, and most definitely, in the small lush island in the Caribbean he believed to be uninhabited.

Six years after Verrazano visit to our area, Henry Hudson first surveyed our shores and local rivers. During his 1609 search for a northwest passage to Asia, Hudson claimed these lands for the Dutch. Although he was an Englishman, he was under contract with the Dutch East India Company, as a result whatever he discovered belonged to the Netherlands. Hudson is credited with being the first European to sail the Hudson river as far as Albany, as well as being responsible for the settling at New York City. Records show him to be good navigator, but lacking in human management skills. He treated crew poorly, had favorites, was head strong, and unyielding. Consequently, mutiny or threats of mutiny ensued on all his voyages.

Both the Captain's log and the diary of his first mate, Robert Julet, describe an arduous journey across the Atlantic, and a difficult and trying exploration of our northern shore. Both describe issues of illness, inadequate provisions, constant threats of mutiny, not to mention recurring conflicts with the native Americans. Hudson at times feasted and traded with the native Americans, and yet at other times clashed violently with them, and often looted their villages.

The Lenape were awestruck by the vivid colors of the *Halve Maen (Half Moon)*, as she sailed the inlets and bay. At first, they traded and even offered food to the crew. The two groups alternated between drinking and feasting together, and the next day one would attack the other without provocation.

In a subsequent voyage, Hudson would discover the great bay in Canada named in his honor. It was here in 1611 his ship, *Discovery,* a ship he owned personally, became trapped in the ice that winter. His crew mutinied, setting him adrift in a small open boat with his son and few other loyal crew. They were never seen or heard from again. Ironically, this same mutinous crew of the *Discovery* was cleared of both mutiny and murder charges.

It is not surprising that with such an unjust end that the spirit of Hudson may not be at rest. Some insist that Hudson is doomed to sail the seas for eternity looking for the justice denied him when his crew was acquitted of the mutiny. Sightings of a phantom *Halve Maen* are seen across the Atlantic, mostly in tempestuous seas, and always without an observable crew.

Through the years there have also been numerous sightings of the antiquated ship, by boaters and yachtsmen. These sights have occurred as far south as Delaware and as far north as Newfoundland. They claim to see an old wooden ship with three masts and faded paint grappling with wild ocean waves. There is never a sign of a crew, the ship does not respond to hailing from others crafts, and it disappears quickly into a stormy night. This includes numerous yachts, recreational boats, three cargo ships, and one coast guard cutter, whose crew does not wish to be identified.

Other reports from the Inuit of the Arctic report that preceding particularly severe winter storms the apparition of Hudson and his fated crew is seen sailing frantically across the ice pack. The men are huddled together for warmth and do not respond to the presence of others. Although it is usually seen at a distance, it is obvious that the manifestation is hovering slightly above the ice. The Inuit use it as a sign to hunker down for the impending blizzard.

Perhaps the best-known legends associated with Hudson comes from the Catskill Mountains. It is true local folklore recorded over many centuries by a multitude of parents and grandparents. According to his journal, Henry Hudson realized on September 3,1609 that the river was not the hidden passage to the East. He turned his ship around and headed back downstream. They anchored for the night near Albany in the shadows of the Catskill Mountains.

After darkness fell the crew heard music coming from somewhere in the forest. Hudson took a handful of men and went in search of the peculiar sound. The farther into the mountains they travelled the louder it became. They came to a clearing where they found an amazing sight. There, singing and dancing about a roaring fire, was a group of short gnome-like people. They had huge oversized heads and pig-like eyes. Their bodies were squat and they all wore long curly beards. Hudson took them to be the community of people that a native American tribe had told them about. The native Americans had called them "the metal working ones".

The small folk welcomed Hudson and his crew to their gathering and offered them food and drinks from tiny cups. Miraculously, no matter how much the sailors drank, the cups were never empty. Soon the crew was dancing and singing with the gnomes. They began a game of ten pins and soon a tournament of sorts filled the air with laughter and sound of crashing wooden pegs.

After a while and many drinks later, Hudson looked around the campfire and was shocked to see that everyone there had huge oversized faces, and were short and squat. When he searched the crowd to find his crew he was shocked to see that some of the gnomes were his crew members. Their heads were swollen to twice their size, their eyes were pig like, and they were as short as their hosts, the gnomes.

Hudson approached the chief with this concern but the leader just laughed and told him that the condition was caused by the magical brew they had ingested. He insisted that the effects were temporary and would disappear when the effects of liquor wore off. He added that it was likely the men would have terrible hangovers.

This left Hudson very uneasy so he gathered up his crew and hustled them back to the ship. They were put to bed immediately and everyone slept late the next morning. When they awoke, they were back to their normal size and appearance. The only residue was a roaring hangover head-ache that lasted three days. Without delay, Hudson set sail and continued down river. By October fourth he had reached the bay and headed home.

Another claim out of New York harbor is that during periods of in-clement weather the phantom of the Halve Maen is seen floating aimlessly amid the choppy waters. The colors are faded on the old wooden ship, but many declare they saw her nameplate, Halve Mean.

There are multiple sights of Hudson and his ship along Sandy Hook bay as well as the Hudson River. One local fisherman recounts his encoun-ter one afternoon while fishing on the bay highlands. He had been on the water most of the day, but when he saw a storm gathering he began to pack up his gear. He took one more glance across the shoreline and there to his surprise was an old ship. It was moving against the tide, although its sails were tightly lashed to the mast. As the ship grew closer, now just 50 yards away he could see that it was a very old ship. It was wooden, had three masts, and the colors on her side were chipped and faded. He shouted and waved to the craft but there was no response, nor was there any evidence of crew on board. It was then that he saw that her keel was exposed, and the vessel was moved through the air just a few inches above the surface of the water.

We must remember that it was here at the site of our two rivers and along our shores that Verrazano and Hudson first encountered native Americans. It cannot be surprising that a huge volume of negative energy and displaced spirits linger here, even today. Ask those who hike the local Henry Hudson trail in late summer, or moor off the Highlands coast. Many will share their uncanny encounters with the specters of Hudson and Verrazano.

Hundreds of centuries have passed since the European explorers first came to the New World. When we inspect their lives, and especially their deaths, we cannot help but note that these "boys" did indeed have bad luck. No matter how you look at it, being beheaded, eaten by cannibals, or dying slowly of disease, is not how a hero expects to die. So, it may be fair to say these are indeed, "bad luck boys."

On the other hand, if we were indigenous to this land, we would likely have a very different perception. We might call them "bad news boys," for their coming was indeed very bad news for the local American natives. Can you picture how you might react if an overwhelming, strange creature appeared without warning, and began destroying all you owned? Would you welcome an invader who thought nothing of killing, kidnaping children, raping, looting, and spreading unknown diseases? We might react just as the native Americans did. What emotions would rise from within? What energies would be released? Would the souls of our slaughtered families ever rest? Could their spirits possibly ever be at peace?

This is our inheritance whether we like it or not. These restless spirits and angry energies reside here with us, just as they have with our ancestors, and just as they will with our descendants. They are now part of who and what we are, part of what we believe, and part of what we fear.